IN THE DAY, DARKNESS

A Novel

A V IAIN

DIII

Friendship. Wilderness. Deception

Wasps Nest

As *the early-morning*, midsummer daylight splashed over the surface of Loch Monar, I could hear my heart thumping in my eardrums. I could feel the dryness at the back of my throat: a reminder from the night before. The many, many beers I'd thrown back. And the, not-so-few, chasers.

Rum, vodka . . . there had been some gin in there too, if I wasn't mistaken.

Not particularly ladylike behaviour.

No wonder my head was a mess.

No wonder it felt as if my brain was attempting to squelch itself out through my ears.

No wonder I had a strange, unshakable sense of guilt.

I splayed my bare toes into the finely ground, rusty-brown pebble beach. Scrubbed the soles of my feet. It felt cool, and the stones massaged the frayed muscles, nerves, tendons . . . and whatever else there is to massage Down There.

The gentle, Scottish sunlight streamed over my skin, making

my already-golden tan glisten a little, as if I might have something magical in my bloodstream.

I breathed in the air. Impossibly fresh. Despite how bad I felt inside, the fragrance of the Scots pines hung over everything.

This was what life was about.

What it was *all* about.

As I leaned back on my elbows, wearing only my mismatched bra-and-panty set—white, bottom; black, top—I thought about one of the many pieces of mother-daughter advice my mum had dispensed to me before coming up here, on this camping trip:

Be sensible, Charlotte.

Yeah, and I'd just about crunched a whole new set of wrinkles into my brow during *that* conversation. It was like the two of us—my mum and me—inhabited wholly different planes of reality. Whereas my mum was this born-again Christian, with a whole range of puritanical baggage to go with it, I had decided, at the tender age of seventeen, that I was going to find out what I liked—what I *didn't* like—all by myself.

And, by twenty-one, I hadn't seen any reason to shift on that thinking.

The reasons for my mum's quickie-conversion were never directly explained to me, but it wouldn't be too difficult to piece the puzzle together.

Since I was only about seven or eight at the time when everything came to a head, I only have vague memories. But vague memories will do:

The strange smell on Mummy's breath.

The sleeping-in late.

And then, of course, the driving ban.

Even a seven-year-old can work out what's right, and what's wrong, when it comes to their own Mummies and Daddies. And especially when 'Mummy' can no longer come and pick you up from school herself for reasons which remain mysterious . . . until one day said seven-year-old discovers an opened letter, carelessly unfurled on the kitchen table, and decides to put her increasingly honed reading skills to use. You don't have to understand all the Big Words to get the Big Picture.

One of the biggest reasons behind mutual-misunderstanding worldwide has to be the concept that parents can know every-thing about their children while, at the same time, believing that the more sordid elements of their lives are kept a secret from their precious offspring.

Not so . . . not *so* at all.

Oh, sure, kids might not know the exact *details* of just what's going on, but, like I said, kids have a way of figuring things out. They have to *live* with those self-same parents after all.

All the smugness.

All the condescension.

The complete package.

But it's just a mask.

A mask to hide the Big Bad World.

No wonder we're all so fucked up . . . and each generation becomes even more fucked up than the one before it.

In fact, I believe that it goes to explain *everything* about the world.

Maybe I should've gone with philosophy as my university subject rather than geography.

Then again, if I had done, I don't suppose it would've brought me here, to the middle of the wilderness of the Scottish Highlands. On a so-called 'fieldtrip'. No doubt, if I'd gone and studied philosophy I would've ended up going somewhere like Athens, or maybe I'd have just spent a great deal of time down the library. Yeah, that never was my *thing*.

"Morning, Charlie."

A groggy, half-asleep voice behind me.

I turned to look.

Eric emerged from the once-purple—*now-pink*—tent we had shared the night before.

It was an old-style canvas tent.

When I first set eyes on Eric's tent, I put it to him that his grandparents had, no doubt, conceived his parents in it sometime in the forties, or fifties. He only scowled and me and said, if I'd known anything *at all* about tents then I would've known that it was from the *seventies*.

'Built to last,' that was how he'd put it, in that tight, Edinburgh accent of his.

The joke was on me, in the end, when I got turfed out of my tent last night.

Eric wore only a pair of bright-red boxer shorts. His chest was bare and his bellybutton was an innie rather than an outie; something which I hadn't experienced before he'd had the good grace to disrobe himself in my presence. His greasy, shoulder-length black hair sort of hung down about the sides of his face like a mechanic's rag that'd been savaged by his pet pit bull.

From somewhere, he produced a pack of cigarettes. He flipped the top, tugged one out with his lips and then lit it up with a lighter he kept concealed in the lid of the carton. He breathed in deeply, and then sighed the smoke out all over the landscape. He turned to me. "Nice day, huh?"

I paddled my hand in front of my nose, warding away the smoke. "It was before the industrial revolution arrived."

Eric smirked at me, then turned his back.

He puffed away, making a show of blowing the smoke in the opposite direction.

"Shame we haven't got any weed left—that'd sort this thumper of a headache I've got going on." He reached up and caressed his forehead, then turned back to me. "How about you, not got any?"

"Nope," I replied.

We'd spread the weed between us all evenly; each of us with an eighth. My bag had been one of the first to go on the trip, in fact . . . it made me wonder if all the fuss about marijuana causing memory loss was more than just alarmist propaganda.

He rolled his eyes, puffed on his cigarette some more. "God, check me out, huh? Some drug dealer I am . . . just about managed to get us a half."

I glanced back behind us, to the other two tents which stood alongside our own.

Both of those tents were from this century . . . which was to say the twenty-*first* century.

One was a leafy-green colour; the one inside which, until the previous night, I'd quite happily rested my weary head. The other tent was a rich brown.

Both seemed to fit in infinitely better with our surroundings than the *pink* monstrosity.

The other two tents were still very much asleep.

Perhaps there was some silent fumbling going on.

That was the most likely eventuality.

One of the worst-kept secrets of our backpacking trip into Deepest, Darkest Scotland had been the love hexagon going on. The way it had worked itself out, six of us had decided to team up for the final-year project. We'd all decided to take a survey of Loch Monar which we'd put together once finished. Against all odds, the project had actually gone reasonably well. We'd got what we needed to get done. The night before hadn't been some all-out hedonistic celebration *for the hell of it* but a very much deserved one. In effect, we'd—all of us—finished off our project.

All that remained was the analysis which would take most of our final year.

Our final year which started up in autumn, at the University of Inverness.

The plan, this morning, was to pack up camp and to head back to the car. Once back at Inverness, we'd all go our separate ways. Me, of course, *I* would simply cross town and go home to my mum and dad who would be waiting patiently for me. I brought them into mind, the two of them slouched up on the sofa—my dad on his back, head in my mum's lap—while the TV chattered on inanely in the background.

The issue with the love hexagon—or whatever shape it'd end up being—had been that me and Eric had both had our respective eyes on certain members of the opposite sex.

I—*Charlie*—had been having lustful thoughts about Graeme; a rower with buzz-cut hair and impossibly *ripped* muscles from Oxford.

Meanwhile, Eric had had a girl called Mercy—*really*—in his sights.

She had mousy-brown hair, a small nose, and those hamster-like cheeks that, apparently, drive all the boys so wild. I suppose that the southerner accent was the straw that broke the camel's back; that vaguely posh, *Queen-like* dialect.

At least that was how it sounded to me.

Needless to say, both me and Eric had thought that this trip would be the perfect opportunity for us to get what we were looking for . . . however, fate has a nasty habit of laughing in the face of all the best-made plans.

In the end, last night, the apparently mutual *liking* between Mercy and Graeme took on physical form. Whereas I'd shared the green tent with Mercy throughout the trip thus far—as insufferable as it sounds—last night, with the romantic lubricant that is alcohol, the two of them had decided to *shack up* . . . which'd left me sharing with Eric.

If I had to pick one lasting memory to settle on from the night before, it would be the scent of wet dog; which was what Eric's tent smelled like . . . oh, that, *and* the sound of 'fumblings'.

Even humming with alcohol, I couldn't help but picture myself as some sort of a benevolent, smiling Grandma staring up at the ceiling of my tent, listening to Eric—my long-suffering husband?—snoring away.

Contrary to popular belief, sharing isn't the cure for heartbreak.

Still, I had the alcohol to thank for blocking out the more pessimistic of my thoughts.

I turned my attention back to Eric, seeing that he'd finished his cigarette.

Being the conscientious geography students that we were—all ecologically minded, and that—he had replaced the jabbed-out butt of his cigarette in the carton.

He gave me a droopy-eyed smile, and said, "Going for a swim —wanna come?"

I thought about playing the Grandma Card . . . saying *no* . . . but, in the end, I rushed on into the freezing-cold freshwater without too much of a fuss.

———

In a strange way, the freezing-cold water of the loch was just what my rapidly developing hangover required. It seemed to stop those uncomfortable stomach spasms; to put paid to the worst of the jabbing pain at my temples.

As I sat on a smooth, large, underwater rock—shale, as I'd discovered earlier in our trip—I stared at the shore of the loch, to our tents pitched there, just before the copse of Scots pines. I saw the pair of bin bags slouched up against the tents, filled with castoff bottles and cans from the party the night before, and I couldn't help but smile at how, even when off our faces, we'd been conscientious enough to dump all our 'empties' into those plastic sacks.

My eyes moved along the shore, and I thought that Eric had at least had the good sense to pitch his seventies tent beneath the range of those swooping branches, in the name of protecting the tent from the worst of any downpour.

It didn't seem like the tent would survive so much as a heavy bout of drizzle.

But then, that was another thing, we'd had just about the best luck possible with the weather.

Despite being warned, by just about every local who came across our path—in thick, Highland accents—that we'd get a 'good washing' on our trip, the entire week had been completely dry . . . not so much as a spot of rain. As I towelled myself off, though, having decided that I'd had enough of the freezing-water hangover cure, I noticed that there were some distinctly soggy-bottomed looking clouds looming large on the horizon.

Still, it hardly mattered that we'd get a drenching on the way back.

We'd be in Inverness by nightfall.

Back with hot showers.

And *microwaves*.

As the goose pimples spotted my skin, I realised that I must've been still feeling the warming glow of the alcohol when I'd been sat on the shore of the loch in only my underwear. Right now, though, I could feel the air cold, crisp.

I ventured back into Eric's tent and dug out my jeans and t-shirt which were screwed into a ball at the foot of my sleeping bag. I thrust both on, and then squeezed my mud-encrusted walking boots onto my feet. Despite it not having rained this week, my boots were still covered in dried mud from some unre-membered expedition in the past. I suppose that a more diligent owner might've got down on their hands and knees with a tooth-brush to bring them to a shine, but, to be honest, I had better things to do than clean boots.

Once I'd got myself dressed, I looked around for Eric. Since there was no mobile phone signal on the loch the only means of entertainment—besides the battery-powered radio Graeme had brought along to listen to the football scores—was conversation.

When I'd first gone into the trip, thought about the trip, I had been mildly horrified by the idea that none of us would be able to contact the outside world; that we'd no longer be hooked up to the World Wide Web twenty-four-seven in the way in which we were accustomed. After the first day of trekking, though, it'd become quite liberating. And by nightfall of the second, when we'd all sat down on the shore of the loch, each with a can of slightly warm beer in hand, I'd decided that we'd actually—somehow—stumbled across a slender slice of paradise.

Whoever knew it'd be in Scotland?

As I stood on the shore of the loch, enjoying the sight of the sun cresting the hills, I smoothed out the wrinkles in my simple, black t-shirt. I'd worn it on the first day of the trek and it'd been smushed at the bottom of my backpack for the duration of our stay here—on Loch Monar. Since today was the day we were heading home, and assuming that everyone else would be feeling just as bad as I did, I didn't think that anybody would notice the smell and/or the less-than-pristine way I'd turned myself out. And, in any case, it really didn't matter any longer.

Graeme had shacked up with Mercy the night before

Just who was I trying to impress?

. . . Certainly not Eric.

That said, I still yanked on a zip-up fleece—also black—over the top.

But I told myself, even then, that it was more for the morning chill than for any kind of illusion of cleanliness or style.

When I looked beyond the green tent, I wondered if I was trying to get a look at the interior. Perhaps I had some sort of masochistic desire to punish myself somehow. To *make myself* see that I'd been a real fool to imagine my fantasies featuring Graeme might have had the remotest possibility of coming true. That he had only ever had eyes for Mercy . . . to put a nineteenth-century slant on the thing . . .

Once I was done with my perving on the green tent, I shifted my attention to the brown one beyond. The tent which the Young Lovers—as Graeme and me had termed them—had shared for the entirety of the trip.

Alex and Petra.

They'd been together since the first week of university.

From what I understood, they had both had a girlfriend and boyfriend, respectively, before they'd got to university. For Alex, he'd had a girlfriend back in Liverpool—his hometown—while Petra had had a lover boy back in Warsaw, Poland, where she was from. As with all 'fateful' meetings, I have no doubt that it was slicked along with no small amount of alcohol and thumping bass . . . but never mock a successful combination, it brought the two of them together.

And they *stayed* together.

At least from my experience it is something of an anomaly for a boyfriend and girlfriend to run the gauntlet and get through to —*almost*—the final year.

Then again, I suppose there *was* still a year to go.

"Charlie . . . Charlie . . ."

I glanced about, hearing Eric's voice.

I didn't catch sight of him for a good few moments.

An almost ghostly thrill passed through my blood.

No doubt Eric's intention had been to shake me up a little.

Finally I spotted him, off among the Scots pines; half-obscured behind one of the trunks.

He jerked his head to one side, indicating that I should follow him.

I looked back to the camp.

To the Young Lovers . . . and then to the green tent with Graeme and Mercy. No doubt they were still locked in one another's arms. I ventured off up towards him.

———

There was no path, of course, only the stomped-down bracken and heather. I breathed it all in, still not quite able to believe it was real. I supposed I'd become so accustomed to respiring that odour in some sort of fabricated fashion that I'd always, for one reason or another, associate it with the small, clear, plastic bottles of car air freshener that're sold on the counters of petrol stations.

Eric moved quickly up the steep slope. He wore a pair of waterproof khaki shorts which, I couldn't help but notice, had a hefty tear right down the crest of his bottom.

I could see the bright-red boxer shorts he wore underneath.

From somewhere—perhaps on the trek here—he had foraged a nice, smooth branch which he'd fashioned, apparently with a pocket knife, or similar, into a perfectly serviceable walking pole; complete with smooth indentations for his fingers.

He used it now to help himself on up the weaving path through the trees.

A couple of times, I felt the pine needles stick me, passing right through the fabric of my fleece and jabbing me painfully in my skin.

As I walked, I felt myself begin to perspire slightly; beads of sweat oozing out of the skin between my shoulder blades, collecting there before rolling down my back.

It just went to show that even a week out in the wilderness wouldn't be enough to whip my body into shape. Then again, I suppose the fact that I hadn't taken a break from drinking might've had something to do with it.

We got through the copse, and up onto the part where the steep slope began to level out.

I turned back to look over my shoulder a couple of times, to look back over Loch Monar, and to see the beautiful stillness of the place. I knew that once I got back to Inverness it would be a shock; and although the city was hardly a metropolis, it would be strange enough to see tarmac again. To see cars crawling about the streets. Buses thundering along.

In some small way, I hoped there might be something I could do to extend my stay out there, in the wilderness.

The mystery of *why* Eric had brought me all the way along this path, all the way up through the Scots pines, to this exact spot, soon became apparent. He strode his way up to a solitary Scots pine, standing out among the flattened-heather.

He turned back to me, a smile tweaking the corners of his mouth. "Want to have some fun?" he said, and then his eyes wandered upwards.

I followed his gaze, and saw that the spot on the trunk which he focussed on was what looked like a large, muddy growth. I squinted, wondering if I should get my eyes checked when I got back to civilisation . . . perhaps a pair of glasses would do me good; give me a fresh start. Geek-chic *was* coming back into fashion, after all . . .

"What is it?" I replied, finally willing to give in.

Grinning all over the place, he replied, "Wasps nest."

" 'Wasps nest' ?"

Eric wiggled his eyebrows in a way I supposed he believed to be endearing, but which struck me as being extremely creepy.

I cast my gaze back down into the valley, down to the loch. I felt a stiff, cooling, morning breeze carry up through the Scots pines. It felt much chillier than at any other time during our field-trip. Those clouds on the horizon were beginning to look extremely ominous.

A storm was coming.

"And what about it?" I said, turning back to Eric.

But he said nothing in reply, he simply thrust his index finger up in the air as if he had just had some sort of masterful idea. Without further explanation, he reached out, took hold of the bark of the tree with his calloused hands. I watched on as he, rather clumsily, set the sole of his boot on a knot which protruded from the bark. He bent his knees and then thrust himself upwards, grabbing haphazardly to a branch which stuck out.

Somehow—I don't *quite* know how—he gripped tightly to the branch.

Heaved himself upwards.

As he helped himself up onto the branch, sitting the ripped seat of his shorts on top, he eyed up the next branch along. He puffed out his cheeks and had gone red in the face.

About the same red colour as his boxer shorts.

I distantly wondered just how we'd manage to get Mountain Rescue out here if Eric did happen to topple off that branch and break his neck. Maybe we could start a signal fire . . .

Eric clambered up the few remaining branches. I estimated that he was about ten, maybe twelve, metres up. About halfway along the height of the tree.

He brought himself level with the nest, clasping the trunk with his knees. Then he made a grab for the wasps nest. It came away easily in his hands.

For a heart-stopping moment, I was certain that he was going to shout, "Catch!" and toss it down at me. But, instead, still using his knees to hold himself to the trunk, he drew the wasps nest in close to his chest, and, from the back pocket of his shorts, produced a tea towel which he wrapped about the nest.

I had to admit that I was somewhat impressed by his antics.

I've always had something of a soft spot for 'brave' male acrobatics.

Even if it was *only* Eric.

Using only his knees, and his free hand, he shimmied his way down the trunk.

Landed with a *thump* before me.

He grinned. "Would've been a mite easier if I'd had my hatchet from back at the camp, but, whatever, no biggie, right?"

"You know," I said, looking to the wasps nest wrapped in the tea towel, "that act of heroics would've been a lot more impressive if you weren't wearing that stupid smile."

But I realised that I was smiling too.

"Come on," Eric said, turning his back to me. "Let's go have some fun."

———

I followed Eric back down through the copse, and to the shore of the loch.

The entire time, I must've held my attention on the wasps nest which he clutched to his chest wrapped in the tea towel. I was wondering what he had in mind, still somewhat stunned by the feat he'd pulled off with that tree-climbing act of his.

Although I thought I'd known Eric reasonably well at university, I'd never have pinned him as being one of those to go down the gym; but, then again, I never would've pinned him as the outdoors type either.

Maybe I just wasn't any good at reading people.

That could *well* have been it . . .

Although I might not have previously known *those* particular things about Eric, I did know of his penchant for practical jokes. I'd heard about the time when he, and half a dozen cohorts, had broken into another boy's room. They had taped all the furniture to the ceiling.

And then there had been the time when they'd—according to my sources—somehow escorted a cow into their halls of residence and then set it to pasture on the lawn outside . . . the local farmer and police hadn't been amused about that one; and, I suppose, they'd been even less amused when the campus CCTV hadn't been able to conclusively demonstrate the identities of those responsible.

From what I'd heard, and this was only gossip, Eric had friends who worked in campus security. I wouldn't think that they'd be beyond 'dealing' with that sort of incriminating evidence for a pal. Although I've never been much for computers, I'm certain that there exists an easy method for obscuring tape *en mass*.

In many ways, Eric was an enigma, although I suppose that *most people* in the world remain that way. At least to me.

When we got through the trees, Eric crouched down, sheltering the wasps nest as he did so. I could tell, just from staring at the back of his head, that he was grinning from ear to ear. He— quite simply—couldn't get enough of this.

That was the first time when I felt something akin to terror.

It was my utmost belief that he was going to unzip the green tent which Mercy and Graeme shared. Toss the nest inside.

And yet, wouldn't that have been so obvious?

After all, like my own case with Graeme, he had never spoken so much as a word about his infatuation with Mercy. Not yet. It seemed wrong for him to commit such an obvious act of jealousy . . . no matter how deliciously *satisfying* it might be for me to witness.

However, he prowled on by the green tent, leaving the fledgling lovers to . . . whatever it is that fledgling lovers get up to . . .

He ventured on to the brown tent.

The one which Alex and Petra shared.

Almost unconsciously, I gave a shake of my head.

I willed him back.

For him not to take another step towards that tent.

He was down on his haunches now.

As if he'd read my mind, he glanced back over his shoulder to me.

That same *wicked* smile smeared across his lips.

Maybe I could've said something—changed his mind.

Stopped him from unzipping the tent.

From hurling the wasps nest inside.

But it was too late.

When I turned to look again I expected to see Eric come hurtling past me, laughing his head off. Perhaps he would be giggling in an out-of-control manner.

But, instead, he remained exactly where he was—down on his haunches.

His complexion had gone quite pale.

I waited for the punchline.

But it never came.

Murder

"*Eric?*" *I said*, a slight bounce in the tone of my voice. Seventy percent fear, thirty percent hysteria. "What is it? What's going on?"

Eric just stayed still.

His eyes locked on the sight within the tent.

From within the tarp, I heard a dull and distant *hum*.

Acting on instinct, I broke free of my static position, trudged up to Eric and then grabbed hold of his arm, by the crook of his elbow. "Come *on!*" I said. "You've . . . done . . . *it!*"

But Eric wouldn't be budged.

He just kept on staring in through the tent flap.

And so I followed his gaze.

At first, I only saw the first few wasps buzzing on out of the tent.

Despite my expectations, they seemed none to miffed about the fate of their home. That their nest had been unceremoniously plucked from its tranquil spot and thrown into chaos. The wasps almost sleepily hummed up into the sky. Then I turned my attention back downwards again.

And to the bare soles of Petra's feet.

Funny that I should first focus on the mud and muck ingrained among the calloused skin, but that was where my eyes took me. From there, though, the process was slow, almost as if my feet were lifting me up off the ground, allowing me to hover for a few simple seconds.

My eyes shifted up, through the dizzy wasps, to the girl lying on her back.

I took in her face, the sable hair dyed electric-blue . . . and then the blood.

It was her neck, I think, though I couldn't be sure.

A muscle wrenched my stomach and I turned away.

I made it maybe three steps from the tent before I dropped to my knees on the pebble shore and threw up a good proportion of what I'd consumed the night before.

It wasn't until I'd retched out my guts for a solid few minutes that I heard stirring in the other tent. In the green tent. The one which Graeme and Mercy shared.

"Charlie?"

My eyes were streaming and I could feel the tears rolling down my cheeks from the effort of bringing up all the half-processed alcohol. A shudder gripped hold of me. A profound tremor. When I glanced up, I saw that it was Graeme; that he had emerged from the tent. He was bare-chested and wore a pair of tracksuit bottoms.

My mind hardly able to square the course of events, I at least had the presence of mind to reach up and wipe the back of my mouth with the sleeve of my fleece.

"Well," Graeme said, crossing his arms over his bare torso,

staring down at me. Even then, I took in his ripped abs, his tight pecs. "I guess it goes to show we all have our limits."

It being Graeme, there's no doubt that, if it'd been any other time, any other situation, I would've responded to that humiliating situation with a polite smile.

But, at that exact moment, I could only stare at him.

Graeme's expression shifted, from that slight smirk he'd been wearing, to a look of concern. Wrinkles appeared in his brow. "What's wrong?" he said. "What's happened?"

But there was no need for me to explain because, already, his eyes were skipping on past me and to the brown tent alongside his own.

He seemed to go through the same process as I had; his eyes skimming over the wasps rising from the interior of the tent, before his gaze centred on the up-turned soles of Petra's feet.

When his brain had cobbled together what'd happened, he leaped the few paces to the tent and crouched down, beside the shell-shocked Eric.

Graeme asked Eric all the same questions as he had me.

And he got the same reply.

Just the steady breeze blowing in over the loch.

That frosty edge to it.

And those clouds, all the time, bundling up over us.

Ready to burst.

Mercy, too, stirred from the green tent.

I couldn't help but feel a gnawing sensation in my chest, seeing her there, with her blond hair, and with those *hamster* cheeks. She was wearing the shirt Graeme had had on the day before . . . one of those light-weight, synthetic fabric jobs. It was a chalk-grey colour and came down well below Mercy's waist, almost to her kneecaps.

She cocked her head to one side, and gave me a slightly giddy smile.

As always, her empty-eyed gaze showed me that there wasn't necessarily anybody home.

When she took in the scene unfolding in the other tent, she shifted her expression away from that smile, and to a look of confusion. And then, meeting Graeme's eye, a look of extreme concern.

"What?" she said. "What is it?"

But, like Graeme before her, there wasn't any answer forthcoming.

From either Graeme or Eric.

I could tell the two of them had well and truly slipped into shock now.

For what felt like an hour, or longer, although it might only have been a few seconds, I remained where I was, crouched on the shore; my vision half-blurred, the loch sweeping out before me, and the rocky, rusty-brown beach melding into it.

More than anything else, I wanted to wake up.

Or, maybe, I was waiting to hear a giveaway *cough-cough*.

Petra stirring from her sleep.

There had to be a logical explanation.

For the blood . . . for Alex's absence . . .

It was then that I felt a hand on my shoulder.

When I turned my attention upwards to look, I saw that it was Graeme. "Charlie," he said, his voice throaty now, and sounding as if he might not be far from vomiting himself. "Have you seen Alex anywhere around here?"

I held so still that I thought I could hear the gentle trickle of blood draining from my skull. Finally, I managed to shake my head.

Graeme continued to fix me with his stare.

To keep up his firm grip on my shoulder.

I thought about how long I'd fantasied over those hands of his . . . those *rower's* hands . . . and now, here they were, *touching* me . . . but this was different; everything had been warped; everything had gone *impossibly* wrong . . .

I could hear murmurs now, behind me.

Mercy and Eric speaking.

No doubt they were wondering what they were going to do.

What *we* were going to do.

There was nothing around here . . . nothing for miles.

It seemed as if a lifetime passed before Graeme released me. And when he did I felt impossibly empty. Just me. Staring out over the surface of the loch.

A drop of freezing-cold rain landed on my hand.

Then another.

"I'd go inside," Graeme said, walking away from me.

I remained still another moment, then tilted my head to him. "Sorry?" I said.

"Your tent—go sit in your tent. Otherwise you'll get wet."

"Oh," I replied, my voice fragile.

Distant.

Floating away.

———

I listened to the rain drumming on the cloth canvas of Eric's tent.

I squeezed my knees together tight as I sat in the tent's entrance, staring out over the loch as the ripples from the raindrops shattered the previously perfect surface.

In the distance, I heard a peal of thunder.

It sent a shimmer up my neck.

And across my skin.

The rain hammered down on the toes of my boots. I watched as they made the encrusted mud wet. It slid off the sides of my boots in sodden clumps. It was almost hypnotic how it would loll across the leather surface and then *plop* onto the pebbles of the shore.

I was dimly aware of what was going on around me.

Of the action—or *inaction*—taking place about the brown tent.

Mercy, Eric and Graeme all wore their anoraks. The draw-strings of their hoods tight as they would go, rendering their faces flabby, fleshy circles. Something about their appearance struck a chord. I thought of those shows on TV; the ones which feature the forensic scientists going to the crime scene.

Eventually, when the rain became too heavy, Mercy and Graeme retreated to the tent alongside us. Eric, meanwhile, squeezed into the tent behind me, dripping chilly raindrops with him as he went. He didn't seem to see the problem with stripping off his anorak in the previously dry tent, but, since it *was* his tent, I didn't feel it was my place to say anything.

I sat side-on so that I could see both the loch, the falling rain, and the interior of the tent. Only then, breathing in the fresh air blowing off the surface of the water, could I compare it with the stale, sweaty—dirty-sock stinking—smell of the inside of the tent.

I suppose it *had* been inhabited by a pair of *men* for the best part of a week.

Perhaps, in my drunken stupor, the night before, I should've thought to offer Eric's tent to the lovebirds. Then me and Eric could've slept soundly in a—more or less—clean tent.

It could've been much worse, I could've ended up sleeping in Alex and Petra's tent.

Now, that *really would* have been a bad move.

24

I was just as quick to stifle the laugh which leaked out of my lips as it was to arrive.

In the end, it only came out as a snort.

Hysteria.

Still, Eric noticed.

"You doing all right, Charlie?" he said.

"Hmm," I said, peering out over the loch, not wanting to look at him now.

"You dealing with it, okay?"

I held myself still—took in the dreary greyness all spread out across the loch.

Again, I felt close to laughing. It was all so ridiculous.

This was *all* so ridiculous.

"Yeah," I finally got out, my throat dry.

"Good," Eric replied, "that's good."

It sounded like he was trying to convince himself as much as he was trying to convince me.

I stared out over the water for a long while, and then I turned back to Eric.

"Did you find Alex?" I asked.

Eric met my eye. "I went to go look for him—I took a quick walk about the campsite, but"—he shook his head—"nothing."

My mind seemed to be slowly kneading its way back into life.

Maybe it was because I could focus on Eric's eyes.

"What happened to her?" I asked.

Eric continued to stare at me, his eyes appearing to narrow more and more, his eyelids seeming to droop further and further down over his eyeballs. When he spoke again, his voice was impossibly quiet. From the way he looked now, I couldn't be sure he was even looking at me anymore. But I kept on looking at *him*.

"Have you ever seen a dead body, Charlie?"

I felt my ribcage tighten.

"I mean," Eric said, with a smile which vanished as soon as it appeared, "had you ever seen a dead body before *today*?"

I shook my head.

"Me neither," he said.

And then, because I sensed that he might be close to drifting away; that he might find himself lost in that same daze I myself had become trapped in, I said, "What happened to her? To Petra?"

Eric swallowed hard.

I saw his Adam's apple bob.

He seemed much paler now.

"The hatchet," he said. "The one we brought along—you know, as part of the camping equipment."

" 'The hatchet' ?" I repeated back at him.

Eric seemed to snap out of whatever daze he'd slipped into. His eyes sought out mine. The way he held his palms flat on the groundsheet of the tent made me nervous, as if he might be ready to leap to his feet and to rush out at any second. As if he might be ready to rush at *me*.

When he spoke again, his voice was more lucid, and he seemed much better focussed. "The hatchet we brought along, you know, to cut guy ropes, whatever. It was that one. Small. Jam"—here he paused, brought his fist up to his lips; shook his head—"*Jammed* into her neck."

I sat there, very still.

Then I pivoted all the way into the tent, turning my back on the loch outside, and the rain which continued to come down in sheets. My reply surprised even me. "Why didn't she *scream*?"

Eric continued to shake his head. He sunk his teeth into his knuckles and then replied, "The hatchet . . . he . . . he swung it into her *windpipe*."

The feeling is difficult to describe, but I felt something—deep

26

down inside—go awfully quiet all of a sudden. Like some sort of void had opened up inside my chest.

———

We remained where we were until the rain eased off in the afternoon.

Across the loch, I spotted a pair of walkers; a man and wife. Although I couldn't make them out easily, I was sure that they were in their fifties, maybe sixties. Their spirits appeared undampened by the weather. I wondered if I should call out to them, tell them about what had happened; that Petra had been murdered. But I felt all locked up, as if invisible hands pinched my lips shut. I was incapable. And, anyway, we would be heading back to civilisation. Why would it make any difference who told the police?

It was then that the thought struck me.

I turned to Eric, who was lying on his side, his sleeping bag zipped all the way open so that he could drape it over himself like a blanket. "Alex?" I said. "What if *Alex* comes back?"

Eric remained where he was.

His eyes turned up to mine.

No alarm.

No distress.

"Graeme is out there," Eric said, "*looking* for him."

As if this settled the conversation, Eric turned his attention back to the side of the tent.

Unwilling to allow this to slide, I shook my head. "When're we going back?" I asked. "When're we *going* to tell someone what's happened here?"

Eric didn't answer me.

I decided to prompt him.

"Eric?" I said. "What's going on?"

"Graeme," Eric continued, "he thinks . . . thinks we should wait . . ."

"Wait for *what*?"

"Wait till we know the facts—wait till we have Alex back here."

Unable to believe him, I leaned forwards, grabbed hold of his wrist. "What're you *saying*?"

Reluctant, he looked up at me. "We'll go when we find Alex, okay?"

It was then that I glanced back over the loch. "That couple," I said, "you see them? On the other side of the water?"

If Eric *had* seen them, he certainly gave nothing away. His eyes never left mine.

"If we don't get up—get ready to leave here right away—then I'm going to call out to them . . . ask them to come *help* us."

Eric shook his head. "Listen to me, listen to what we've worked out; the best way to do this."

I squeezed his wrist tighter still, felt that I was digging my fingernails into his skin. If he felt pain—and I'm certain he must've done—then he didn't show it. "What do you *mean* you've worked things out? What do you *mean*?"

"Look, Charlie," Eric said, his voice flat now, "while you were all stuck in that . . . whatever *happened* to you . . . we got talking, and . . ."

This time I brought my hand up and slapped him across the cheek.

Though I'd never slapped anyone before it had felt—in the moment—the only thing that I could do. Almost like a reflex.

Eric smarted at the blow, and raised himself up on his elbows. He reached out for the cheek where I had struck him and pressed his palm tentatively against it.

When I spoke again, my voice was firm, unmoving. "We're going to pack up *now*," I said. "And then we can talk about it— we can talk about it with the *police*."

Eric jabbed his tongue into his cheek. "You know, I think you might've broken a tooth."

"Don't be such a drama queen. You make it seem like it's the first time a girl's hurt you."

Resolved to get the attention of the couple across the water, I shuffled across the groundsheet, and peered back out through the opened flap of the tent.

I could see the two of them, moving in the falling rain, on the other side of the loch. Even with the rigid wind, I was certain that I would be able to catch their attention. They might have something . . . a *satellite* phone?

I had only maneuvered myself onto my knees, ready to thrust myself upwards into a standing position, when I felt Eric take hold of me by the elbow. I tried to shake him off.

He held on firm.

"Let me go!" I said, a slight panic entering my voice.

"Stay, Charlie, be *patient*."

" 'Patient' ?! Petra's *dead*. Eric, there's a murderer on the loose —*Alex*. How the hell am I supposed to be patient?"

"Just, please . . ." Eric's words faded away.

I realised I could hear footfalls outside the tent.

The crunch of the pebble beach beneath the sturdy soles of walking boots.

I felt Eric's grip slacken, but my thoughts of calling out to the couple on the other side of the loch had dwindled. All of a sudden it didn't seem to be such an urgent matter . . . or maybe it was just because something more pressing—*more dangerous*—had come up.

The voices were muffled, and when I peered out through the

tent flap, to the rain still drooling down, I realised I could no longer see the couple on the other side of the loch. They had, most likely, vanished behind one of the folds in the land.

Out of nowhere I heard a scream.

A *male* scream.

My whole body seized tight.

It felt as if my blood was on fire.

My heart leaped up to my throat.

As I settled back down, listened to the echo of the scream bouncing back from the other side of the loch, it surprised me to feel Eric's lips almost touching my ear, to feel the moisture on his breath as he spoke in a whisper. "Charlie, for your own sake, just be calm. Okay?"

For my own sake?

What was *that* supposed to mean?

———

About ten minutes later, the sun was out and shining. I felt it warm my cheeks, bring me out in a slight sweat beneath my fleece. Four of us—*the survivors*—were standing on the shore of the loch. Gathered in a circle. No one else around. No sign of the couple from earlier. I supposed that most other potential day-trekkers had taken one look at the cloud cover that morning and called off whatever expeditions they might've been planning.

I looked from Eric, standing beside me, to Graeme, next along in the circle.

Finally, I turned to Mercy.

Over by the shore I could make out Alex, hunched up, staring into the clear water of the loch. Thinking about *who knew* what . . .

I was glad to feel that the attention had been drawn away

from me; that the focus of the group was now on Alex, who I could see, even in profile, was a terrible shade of pale. And that tears rolled down his cheeks. He clutched his hands at his stomach and seemed ready to vomit at any moment.

"Where'd you find him?" Eric said, to Graeme.

All of us seemed aware that the function of the circle was to block Alex out; to speak in private without him overhearing.

Graeme met my eye for a moment. I felt an odd, sizzling-hot sensation in my gut briefly. Then he turned to look at Eric. "Over there," Graeme said, flapping his hand at some spot in the distance. "He was doing what he's doing right now." He shook his head, dropped his voice, even though it didn't seem like Alex was at all interested in what he had to say. "Staring into the water."

"Did you . . ." Eric continued, and then drifted off. "I mean, you think that he was in the water, to clean the blood off his hands?"

Although Graeme shrugged, his eyes sunk back in their sockets, the sheer revulsion obvious to all of us. "Maybe," he said, "I didn't see any blood on him—nothing on his clothes." He paused, drew breath, and I realised that Graeme must've been feeling as queasy as I did. "But I'm no expert . . . I'm sure his fingerprints are all over that hatchet."

At that moment, a wild wind whipped through the Scots pines. I drew in the heady scent of nature. It sent a chill dancing along my spine, made my heart dip down to my stomach. There was something about being out here, in the middle of nowhere, which made it seem as if all the old rules simply didn't apply.

There were no police out here.

No telephones, even.

It'd be a full day's hike back to the cars.

"Look," I said, surprised that I'd plucked up the strength to speak—I caught Mercy's eye for a fraction of a second and saw that she was just as surprised at my sudden contribution, "this is nothing to do with us—we have to go to the police; tell them what happened." I shook my head. "I don't know what all this is about, *why* we're stalling." As the breeze blew over the loch again, I wrestled with my tangled, honey-coloured hair, and tucked it back behind my ears. "If we set off now—*pack up now*—then we'll be back at the cars before nightfall. We might even get some signal on our phones on the way back."

"My phone's dead," Eric contributed.

I rolled my eyes, but held myself from saying anything out loud, knowing that my phone was equally out of battery. I suppose the temptation to fire up the odd app—here and there—had proved too much to resist. And, over the course of a week, with no means of charging up, it'd run down my phone's charge. Looking to Mercy and Graeme, I was certain it was the same for them.

Still, it didn't matter.

We'd already wasted a good hour, or more, waiting about here.

It would make little difference to the timing if we called from our phones, or from the village where we'd parked up the cars.

When I turned back to the group, to see how they might react, I saw that something was troubling Graeme. Since Graeme was one of those who didn't mind speaking at any opportunity, it took only the merest of glances from me to get him talking. "There was one thing," he said.

"What?" I replied.

Graeme glanced to Eric, to Mercy, and then to me again. "On the way back from the loch, Alex was muttering something about a 'break-up' . . . that he and Petra had *finished* things . . . when I brought him back here, well, you know . . . you heard that *scream* of his, right?" Graeme's eyes twitched about their sockets, as if he was having difficulty in knowing where he should look next. "It was like this was the first time he saw her—the first time he saw Petra *dead* . . ."

As silence loomed over the loch, I couldn't help but put in, "Perhaps it was the first time he saw her dead—*sober*."

For some reason I felt a ticklish sensation at the base of my ribcage. I'm sure it was shock—my *brain* still processing that someone had *died*.

Nobody else thought to pitch in another comment, and, in the end, we all settled on fixing our gaze on Alex, wondering what might've possessed him to do such a thing.

———

Someone—*Graeme?*—had zipped up Alex and Petra's tent so that we wouldn't have to look at her body. So it wouldn't be exposed to the open air. Every so often, a wasp buzzed about the campsite, and I would swat it away from my nose, or chin, or wherever it decided to go *buzz-buzz*.

Seeing that nobody else was getting anything done about returning to civilisation, and getting Alex turned in for what he'd done, I decided to make a start on my own packing.

It wasn't too difficult of a job since everything was already stuffed into my rucksack. In fact, I was a little disappointed that it only took me the best part of fifteen minutes to get everything sorted. It meant I would have to pay attention to the others.

The others were all still moping about.

Alex down by the water, staring into the loch.

Eric was whittling away at the walking stick he had crafted out of wood, while Graeme was doing sit-ups on the periphery of the campsite.

Mercy had cracked open a well-thumbed paperback and was leafing through the pages.

As I took them in, I couldn't quite believe it.

Couldn't *believe* they were acting this way.

While I tried to process them, I couldn't help but think of *Murder on the Orient Express* . . . that, in the end, it'd been *all* of them who had killed the victim.

. . . All of them apart from me, that was.

Was *that* what Eric had been getting at?

When he'd told me to 'be calm for my own sake' ?

I shook that away and, with a determined step, made my way for the trail leading along the shore of the loch. I wasn't an owner of either of the cars so I would simply go to the village, report what had happened and hope that the kind people living in those cottages might call a taxi for me, or let me know about the local bus routes.

However, I only made it as far as Graeme, doing his sit-ups, when he leaped up and blocked my path. "Where're you going?" he said.

In that moment, I didn't feel anything for him at all . . . only a vague annoyance that he was *trying* to make trouble.

"Back to the village—to tell them what happened."

Graeme seemed stumped for a second, and I couldn't help but believe that *he* had to have had a hand in killing Petra. What other motive might he have for blocking my way?

"You can't," he said. "Not yet."

I reached back to the side pocket of my rucksack.

I could feel my pocket knife stashed away there.

Some well-meaning aunt—apparently not wanting to gender stereotype me at such a young age—had given it to me for my seventh birthday. I could still remember hiding the contents of the unwrapped present from my mother so she wouldn't confiscate it.

Later, I can clearly recall drawing the longest blade and running it across my right finger. And, with hot pain, and not a little surprise, watching the blood ooze free from the slit skin.

That blade had since rusted, and the other implements were of limited use as weapons, but Graeme didn't need to know that. The knife would be enough to rattle him.

I worked the side-pocket zip open and slipped the knife free.

I was aware of Graeme's eyes following my hand closely, all the way down to my thigh where I allowed the knife to dangle in my tightly clenched fist.

I felt Eric behind me.

I turned around.

Glanced at him.

Tilted my head to one side and shut one eye in—what I hoped was—a sisterly fashion.

"What, have you gone mental, too?"

Eric just kept up his sombre expression. "What're you gonna do with that knife, Charlie?"

"Nothing," I said, turning away from him, and looking back at Graeme. "Nothing if you let me leave . . . if you let me *go*."

Over Graeme's muscular frame, I caught sight of Alex. He still crouched beside the loch, but now he was staring over at us. I wondered if he was going to attack me, too.

Now that I thought of it, I couldn't quite believe that this could be anything *other* than a conspiracy. That, for whatever reason, Alex had flipped out, killed Petra, and now his two 'buddies' here were trying to cover it up.

Well *I* certainly wasn't going to have any part in this.

I moved quickly, the pocket knife still clenched in my fist.

I bundled forwards a few steps, catching Graeme off guard as I did so. He tripped a couple of times before he finally regained his balance, and that was all I needed to stumble away from them.

And then to break into a sprint.

As I felt my calf and thigh muscles pumping me along the flattened long grasses, I didn't dare so much as look back over my shoulder. But I could hear the *thud* of footsteps pursuing me. Two pairs of footsteps.

I strained myself harder, tasting blood in my mouth, feeling sweat trickle down the sides of my face. My breathing deepened, and I puffed out my cheeks. I felt the burn of my muscles as I clambered my way up the slope, away from the loch, aiming for a copse ahead.

Wanting to escape.

The ground was uneven and I suppose it was inevitable that the two boys would catch me. As I felt my foot sink down into a rabbit hole, concealed by the flattened grass, I struggled to pull it free.

Failed.

I staggered forwards, feeling a twisting, tearing sensation in my ankle.

Before I knew quite what was happening, my head smashed into the moist grass. I flexed my fingers and felt the pocket knife slip out of my hold. It skittered into the grass, surely lost forever.

And then their hands were upon me.

Grabbing me around my wrists.

About my ankles.

"You get that side," I heard Graeme say.

And then they lifted me up.

Carried me back to the campsite.

Maybe I would've struggled more if not for the unbearable pain in my ankle.

An Eerie Afternoon

W*hen I regained my senses*, I was back in Eric's tent.
This time, though, I was zipped inside.

In the dimming sunlight, I could make out Eric's silhouette, slouched-up there, sitting with his back to the flap so that I wouldn't escape.

I was imprisoned.

They'd *made me* a prisoner.

From a combination of my, and Eric's, sleeping bags, I had created a raised cushion where I rested my leg now; where I held my ankle elevated. It felt as if all the blood in my body was pumping into that single joint, filling it up, bringing a nasty welt to the surface of the skin. They'd left me a stainless-steel flask of water . . . at least they weren't going to leave me to die of thirst.

Outside, I could hear speaking: low, gruff tones.

Considering that Eric was sitting 'guarding' the tent, I supposed that it was Alex and Graeme speaking together. What on *Earth* could they be speaking about?

. . . Perhaps they were discussing what they would do with me.

If Alex would do *me* in just the way he had done in Petra.

Even without my rusted-up pocket knife, I fancied my chances at beating him back. Even if all three of the boys came at me, I was determined to fight them off for as long as I could.

No, I was determined to *escape*.

I thought back to the week we had shared together; all the 'normal' activities. The way we would wake up and eat breakfast together, brew up some coffee. There had been a steady daily rhythm to everything. A *calmness* to it all.

But, after just a single night of madness, all that had changed.

Everything had transformed.

And, for all I knew, I would never leave Loch Monar.

Never get to complete the geography project we had all set out here to do.

I listened to the sound of footsteps approaching the tent. The scrub of boots over the pebble beach. I felt an acute tweak of pain in my ankle. My breathing shallowed. And, in that moment, I knew running away from my 'friends' would be much harder than I had considered.

We were in the middle of nowhere.

And, chances were, they wouldn't allow anybody close.

Not close enough even to hear my screams.

The tent flap zipped open.

Ruby-red sunlight flooded in.

Already, the sun was setting on the loch, disappearing behind the rugged hills surrounding.

Alex's face appeared in the gap.

I reached about me.

Fumbling for *something*.

For an *object*.

In the end the only thing which came to hand was the flask of water.

I held it close to my chest, in a defensive posture, clearly ready to use it as a sort of crude club if he got too close to me.

"Charlie?" he said, his voice a little floaty; his Liverpudlian accent cutting through the way he spoke my name. "Can we have a chat?"

I backed up against the side of the tent, and the only word on my mind was, "No" . . . *No, no, no . . . a thousand times, no!*

But I couldn't form the words.

Alex stepped in through the opened flap, and I caught a glimpse of Eric's back as he sat slumped against the outside of the tent.

I kept my eyes fixed to Alex's hands, sure that he would be holding a weapon; that same hatchet which he'd used on Petra . . . or *something else?*

Didn't they say that killers often got bored?

That, mostly, they killed to entertain themselves?

Alex zipped the tent flap shut behind him, at the same time sealing out the sunlight and limiting my hope of escape. I had time to take in his shaggy, strawberry-blond hair. It jagged down about his ears, in need of a good cut. And I looked to those thin, almost China doll-like cheeks of his. And how his spry body seemed capable of manoeuvring into any given shape. He eyed me.

Blue eyes.

A *murderer's* eyes.

"I didn't do it," he said, his tone flat, emotionless.

He almost had me believing that he was telling the truth.

I tried to back away from him a little more, but only came up harder against the tent cloth. "What'd you want?" I said, finally getting something out.

Alex blinked several times.

He sniffed.

His eyes glittered with tears.

He swallowed.

"I had nothing to do with it," he said. "I want you to know that."

"You expect me to believe—"

"Please," Alex said, this time with a whimper in his voice—that, I suppose, was what caught my attention. "I've . . . you don't know . . . now that she's . . . that she's—" He tugged his knees up to his chest and crossed his arms over his kneecaps. He buried his face in the backs of his forearms. His whole body shuddered as he sobbed.

Was this how all murderers got?

When they were denying what they'd done?

Was there some *human* part of them which remained, which *wouldn't* allow them to give in totally to the monster?

. . . It was all speculation.

I had no idea.

Alex remained that way for a few minutes before he finally brought his head back up. "Charlie," he said, "these past couple of years, they've been great, but it's sort of cut me off from the rest of the world, you know?" He shunted his nose with the heel of his hand, snorted a couple of times, and then went on. "The only one I ever talked to was her. And now . . . now she's . . . *gone.*"

This time he managed to speak the word without wavering, without breaking down into sobbing again. I had to admit that I felt something in my chest give—almost a *tender* feeling seize hold of my heart. I had to keep reminding myself that this was all an act.

But, with every second that passed, it got harder and harder to do.

Alex continued, "Last night, I . . . well, we were *all* pissed off our heads, right? We had a fight, a *bad* one . . . don't know how you didn't hear it."

I stretched my mind back, still feeling the numbing effects of my hangover.

It was difficult to draw back the drunken mists of time, but I did my best.

There seemed to be *some* recollection. Perhaps while I was in the loch. I had been submerged up to my neck, keeping my beer can cold; leaving the top to stick out of the surface of the water. I was taking sips. Tiny little sips. Every now and again. And I was alone.

On the shore I saw Alex and Petra, the two of them facing one another.

At first I had waved to them . . . then, thinking they hadn't seen me, I'd called out.

No doubt I'd broken the good night's sleep any of the wildlife might've been having.

It'd been then, in my drunken state, that I'd gauged the fact that Alex and Petra were having some sort of a fight. I could remember clearly that Petra shot off a warning glare in my direction, and, even though I'd felt warm and fuzzy inside, I'd sheepishly returned to my beer can. A few moments later, Petra—blue hair and all—had stalked off.

Away into the trees.

Alex had hesitated on the shore.

But then he had broken free.

Run after her.

That, I supposed, was the fight he'd been referring to.

Alex shook his head, staring at the tent cloth, as if he was replaying this same scene in his own mind. "I went after her, and I looked, but it was dark . . . and she was *hiding*." He turned back to me, the tears rolling down his cheeks now. "In the end, I remember it clearly. I got back to the tent, and I went inside. Then I lay myself down. Fell asleep. When I woke, it was already getting light. And Petra still wasn't there. I was worried, so I went out to go look for her. To go and search for her about the loch. I made it all the way around the shoreline before I just decided to go and crouch and stare into the water. That was where Graeme found me."

I stared hard at Alex, doing my best to work out if there was any sort of expression—any facial tic—which might give him away. But I could see nothing at all . . . only a face steeped in true mourning and regret. He didn't even get a chance to say goodbye.

Or perhaps that was just a lie I told myself.

———

After the meeting with Alex I thought that Graeme and Eric would let me free, but, instead, it was Mercy who stepped past the sentry at the tent flap. She was now stripped down to a black-and-white striped bikini top and a pair of cut-off jeans.

Somehow her dress seemed inappropriate.

As with Alex before, she zipped the tent flap shut behind her.

I was distantly impressed that the others had already begun to establish protocols, and good practice, with regards to their prisoner.

Mercy gave me a weak smile, and I caught a hint of gin on her breath.

I guessed that they'd all been slicking their decision-making along with a little of the 'Devil's tonic', as my mum might've put it.

"Mercy, we need to get the police."

I was surprised at how lucid I made myself sound, despite not having eaten a thing all day. I'd taken to rationing the water, unsure what I should reasonably expect from my 'friends'.

Mercy met my eyes for only a fleeting second.

She lay herself down on her side and started to fiddle with a loose thread in the groundsheet. "You need to stay here for the time being," she said, "till we're sure we can trust you."

"*Trust* me?" I said, a laugh almost in my voice.

Mercy glanced up at me briefly.

Nodded.

Unable to believe what I was hearing, I stretched myself to a feigned chuckle, and felt a tremor of pain dance up the back of my calf from my ankle. I gesticulated wildly, indicating the campsite outside the tent. "You let *Alex* go free and he's the number-one suspect."

"Not anymore."

"What's that meant to mean?"

There was a long, drawn-out silence.

Finally, it dawned on me.

"You think *I* did it? That *I* killed her?"

Mercy remained perfectly still.

I imagined—if she decided to go into law postgraduate, as she'd been threatening—she would make an excellent barrister. Leaving gaps in the hope that the witnesses would fill in missing information. When I went on work experience with the local paper, I spent nearly the entire week in a courtroom, and got to learn those *lawyer* tricks quite well.

Human nature is to be helpful, especially when under threat.

A very useful trait to exploit in the unwary.

I held my breath.

Calmed myself down.

I knew that it *had* to be impossible . . . I had been off doing my own thing, mostly, the night before. Drinking, sure. But I'd never—*ever*—once given the indication of being violent while drunk. Actually, my oddest habits would mostly revolve around, when I got home from a night out, grabbing a vacuum hoover, or getting a head start on my ironing. The fact that the vacuuming would—*inevitably*—miss all the dirtiest of spots, and the ironing would need to be redone in the morning, always seemed to fall by the wayside as far as my drunken self was concerned.

Finally, Mercy deigned to meet my eye. "I didn't kill her," I said, my voice flat, toneless. "And if you're saying that I did then we *definitely* should get the police involved."

Mercy continued to stare back at me. "We're not saying that," she said. "And we *will* go to the police when the time is right. We just want to be sure. We want to make sure that we're not making any mistakes."

" 'Mistakes', how?" I said, wishing more than anything at that point that I'd been privy to whatever conversations they'd been having outside; on the campsite.

"It looks bad," Mercy said.

My eyes almost lolled clean out of their sockets. "Really?" I said, my voice sarcastic, though who knows where *that* came from. "Petra—*our friend*—had her neck chopped in with a hatchet, and you think it looks *bad?*"

Already, Mercy was raising herself up off the groundsheet, hobbling her way on her knees towards the tent flap. I leaned over, feeling as if thousands of searing sparks danced up from my ankle. I grabbed hold of her bare shoulder.

Mercy turned, her eyes wide.

Scared.

"Listen," I said, making my tone of voice more reasonable, "this is nothing to do with us . . . we've got *nothing* to hide . . . when Alex spoke to me"—I shook my head—"I don't know . . . I *believed* him, that he had nothing to do with it. That the first time he saw her dead was when Graeme brought him back to the campsite." I stared deeper into Mercy's eyes. "Is *that* enough for you? Enough for you to *release* me?"

Mercy said nothing in reply, although her eyes drifted down to where I roughly held her arm.

"And *I* certainly didn't have any reason to *kill* Petra—why would *I* do that?"

A slight smile twisted back the corners of Mercy's mouth. "Because you're in love with him."

"What?" I replied.

But Mercy said nothing else, and, a few seconds later, I allowed my grip to go slack.

I let her go.

She unzipped the tent and slipped out.

Before she zipped the tent shut once again, she crouched back down and peered in at me. "The reason that we have to be sure is that, if the police get the wrong idea then we could *all* get into trouble. We could *all* go to prison." She cocked her head to one side. "And that wouldn't be at all fair on the others, now, would it?"

I took one final look at that smug expression of hers. It took everything within me to remain sitting on the groundsheet of the tent. It was a good thing for Mercy that I had a gammy ankle, otherwise I might've convinced myself to tear her to pieces. And to *hell* with guilt or innocence.

———

I didn't really start to take my 'friends' seriously until night fell. Until the bright, fading sunshine was replaced by a staunch, near-complete blackness.

Up in the Highlands, it never quite gets dark during the short summer nights, and it was near enough a full moon that particular night.

I don't know if I expected to remain where I was for the foreseeable future—in solitary confinement. I guess that I had made some sort of peace with the fact because I'd bedded myself down and closed my eyes when I heard the tent flap zip back.

When I turned to look I saw that Eric and Alex were clambering in.

The two of them, even in the moonlight, I could see, had deep, black bags hanging below their eyes. I supposed that Petra was still right where she'd been found, in the brown tent.

They lay down. One on either side of me.

Holding me prisoner.

During the night it rained hard. Even the sound of the rain wasn't enough to cover the constant snores of Eric and Alex. I thought over and over about what I'd heard. About what Mercy had said to me. That I was 'in love' with *him*. Alex, of course, was who she meant.

I've always thought female intuition to be extremely overrated.

. . . If only she knew.

The most perplexing part of it all was trying to work out *how* Mercy had got the idea that I was in love with Alex. What sort of an impression had I given? And, more to the point, how had I portrayed my character in such a way so as to make her think that I was willing to *murder* so that I might possess him. In actual fact I thought that it said far more about Mercy's mind than my own.

As I lay there, feeling my ankle throbbing away, I turned over what Mercy had told me, about them wanting to be 'sure' before going to the police. No matter how much I thought about it, though, I couldn't quite get to grips with what she might mean.

If it was true that Alex *hadn't* killed Petra then who would have done?

I knew *I* was innocent.

But, what about the others?

Was someone else nurturing a secret—keeping the Whole Truth from the rest?

Graeme was the first to pop into my head, for no other reason than wanting to think of someone other than those I shared the tent with. And I'd done enough thinking about Mercy for what seemed like a lifetime. What motive would Graeme have for killing Petra?

. . . Did he have some kind of a bisexual secret to him?

Was it possible that my lust might've acted as a pair of blinders, not allowing me to see the obvious signs; that he'd been pining for Alex all along?

It was only when I reached up to touch my face that I realised I was smiling in the darkness.

Reluctantly I turned my mind to Mercy.

I *knew* for a fact that she had no interest in Alex. I had heard her, on many occasions, making tittering, chippy remarks about how he looked like a 'withered, old ghost' . . . or had that been a simple front? A means for her to hide her *true feelings* . . . it might well have been in some nineteenth-century melodrama, but it just didn't fit here.

Next, having scratched Alex from the list of suspects for the time being, I thought about Eric.

Now it seemed that jealousy was *right* out of the picture. He had made his infatuation with Mercy so obvious that I couldn't see anybody else he *might* be interested in. And if Eric *had* been obsessed with Petra to the point of being willing to murder her—sober or drunk—then *surely* I would have noticed. Or maybe I was giving myself too much credit.

I thought about myself lying there, playing the death of one of my course mates as if it was some kind of a parlour game. But, then again, given my friends' behaviour what was I expected to do?

They were the ones who had made this all a game.

As I tried my best to allow my mind to slip away into the Land of Dreams, I couldn't shake the image of Petra's bare feet from my mind. That electric-blue hair.

And the wasps, one by one, dozily ambling their way out of the tent.

Oblivious.

Wasting Time

When *I first* opened my eyes the next morning, I was certain that I was the first awake.

I looked over the sleeping bodies lying beside me—Eric and Alex—and I was certain that this was the opportunity I had been waiting for.

My chance to escape.

On my knees, I worked as gently as I could to open the zip of the tent flap, wary of making any loud sound that might wake the pair of sleeping princes.

Sure enough, out on the campsite, I saw nothing but the dawning day.

Overcast skies.

Rain in the air.

And, like the day before, not a soul in sight.

I reached for my boots, the pair of them lying haphazard, on their side in the long grasses beside the tent. Sitting on the bare ground, I tugged on one boot, and then went to tug on the other. As I pulled the boot towards me, I felt it become stuck. A severe pain hit. It ran up through my entire body, tightening every muscle, making my breathing become shallow. In the night, it seemed, my ankle had well and truly swollen up.

Made it impossible for me to get it past the comparatively tight-fitting hole in my boot.

I considered my situation, worked it out from all angles.

And then decided to stand up.

That only made the situation worse.

Trying to jam my afflicted ankle into the boot, I felt as if some psychopath was jabbing pieces of broken glass into my skin. Before too long, I simply couldn't take it anymore, and I let loose a low *squeal* of pain. In the end, I settled for simply standing on the boot, using it as a sort of barrier between my socked feet and the bare ground.

However, when I took the first few steps, I realised how fool-hardy of me it was to believe that I would be able to get away from here at all.

Every second step was pure pain.

I sank my teeth into my lower lip in an attempt to mitigate it, but, by the end, it was simply too much for me to bear.

As I allowed myself to drop downwards, onto the ground, I let out an involuntary groan.

A groan which triggered movement in the tent I had just left behind.

Before so much as ten seconds had passed, I caught sight of Eric's face peering out at me through the tent flap. His eyes met mine. There was a sort of apology there. Almost a shame in what he had to do next . . . then again, from my perspective, he had *every reason in the world* to feel ashamed of what he was doing. Of *how* he had treated me thus far.

He ventured out of the tent, and approached me.

From where I sat, collapsed, on the bare ground, I cursed

how easily he slipped on his own pair of walking boots. And then how he approached me with a carefree gait.

When I was a little girl, I fell out of a tree and broke my arm. Even now, I can remember the pure frustration of being physically limited for however long my arm was in that cast. Although it couldn't have been longer than two months, it felt as if it was a decade. It being summertime, and the holidays, had only made it worse. I didn't want that to happen again.

But maybe I should have thought of that before I sprained my *fucking* ankle.

Surprisingly, as Eric approached, I didn't note any malice in his expression.

He was wearing the same pair of khaki shorts he had used the day before—and apparently slept in—along with a chequered, button-up shirt which I'd seen him wear on the first day of the trek.

He stood over me, and looked down at my ankle. "Bad, is it?" he said.

Unable to really address the inanity of the comment, I copped out of it and replied, ". . . Yeah."

Eric nodded, as if he understood all the nuances of the situation now.

Then he gave a vague grin.

"Were you trying to sneak out?"

I tried my best to resist for as long as I could, and then, unable to, I found myself smiling back at him. "Yeah," I said, almost bashful about it.

Eric scratched at the back of his neck and surveyed the loch opening out before us. Then he looked up at the overcast skies above. "In for a bit of rain later on, you think?"

"Maybe."

Eric pouted and nodded again, then he turned back to me. "I

think we'll get everything cleared up today—hopefully we'll be home by tonight."

"Hope so."

A long pause, and then, "Are you all right, Charlie?"

I said nothing.

As if it'd help with my comprehension, Eric got down on his haunches and stared me right in the eye. "Listen," he said, "this's a terrible thing that's happened but we're getting through it together, all right? Once we're through, I promise you'll see it was for the best."

I severely doubted that.

And, to be fair, I was certain that Eric did too.

Right then, though, I felt like I wanted to know more.

That I wanted to get *answers*.

"Eric?" I said.

"Hmm?" he replied, staring out over the loch, as if this was just another normal day up in the Highlands, all of us pitching in to get our project work done.

"Where were you the night before last?"

"The night before last?"

"Yeah."

Although I didn't so much as slip him a sidelong glance, I heard the sharp *scratch-scratch-scratch* of his fingernails rubbing against the dried-up skin at the back of his neck.

"That whole thing," I went on, " with the wasps nest in the morning; that wasn't some sort of *cover*, now, was it?"

Again, a long, unconvincing pause.

"What makes you say that?" he finally replied.

I sneered. "What makes you think *I* killed Petra?"

Another pause.

Then, "I don't know, Charlie, I don't think that *any* of us really know what happened that night."

"One of us does," I replied. "One of us *has* to know. I'm sure the police would be able to find out without too much trouble. That hatchet should have some fingerprints on the handle." I craned my neck up to him, and saw that he was looking out over the water. "Why don't we go to them?" I said. "Why're we playing these games?"

Eric remained silent for several beats, and then said, "I don't know, Charlie."

———

Breakfast was Spartan.

We hadn't brought supplies with us to last much more than the week we'd planned for our project. Believing it was going to be our last day at the loch, we'd gone a bit mad. Eaten up all our remaining provisions. Three slices of bread, a couple of tins of baked beans, was all that remained.

I passed on the bread, seeing that it'd already gone a touch mouldy about the edges, and I didn't eat more than a spoonful of the beans provided.

Despite not having eaten anything the day before, I didn't feel much hunger.

I just wanted to leave.

I wanted to go to the police.

Tell them what had happened.

I wanted the others to see *sense*.

That morning, I noticed a pungent smell clinging to the campfire. At first I thought that an animal had come along in the night and taken a shit against one of the tents. In the end, though, I realised that it was coming from the brown tent. Where Petra's body lay.

I wondered if there was a limit to the time a body might be useful in a murder enquiry.

If—after a certain number of hours—it would no longer give up the evidence it had once offered. And, thinking along those lines, it was difficult not to wonder if one of the others was banking on this assumption . . . hoping that if they left the body long enough they would never get caught.

Or that we would *all* get caught.

That *all* of us would be found guilty.

Once we'd finished with breakfast, and Graeme and Mercy, still on their honeymoon period despite the circumstances, had ventured on down to the shore of the loch to cleanse the pans of bean juice, I turned to the brown tent and said, "How're we going to do this?"

My words were greeted with silence from both Eric and Alex.

I looked to them. "I mean, are we going to leave Petra here while we fetch the police; *trust* that nobody does anything with the body?" I paused, waiting for a response, and seeing that none was forthcoming went on, "Or are we going to take her with us?"

I couldn't help but feel a touch insensitive when I finally caught Alex's eye, saw that he was tearing up again. He crushed his lips together and bowed his head into his chest.

The more that I looked at him—the more I was around him —the more I came to believe that he truly was innocent of any crime.

Or maybe I'm just a sucker for criers.

I looked to Eric, certain of at least getting a response from him.

"Don't they always say that you can't mess with a crime scene?"

"Yeah," I said, flashing my eyebrows, "and I'm pretty certain that they *also* say you should report a crime as soon as you come across one." I glanced to Alex, saw that he was still snivelling to himself, turned back to Eric. "The police can *tell* how long a body's been deceased," I said. "They have *ways* of finding out—and they're going to want to know just what we were doing all this time, when we should've been getting in touch with them. When we should've been doing everything in our power to *get* to them."

Eric remained silent.

I recalled what'd happened the day before, and decided that this might not be the way to go . . . unless I wanted to find myself in solitary confinement again.

"Look, all I'm saying is that we need to get our story straight—like you've been saying all along. If we agree that we're all innocent, then don't you *also* agree that it makes us look *guilty* to be delaying going to the police; for us not to have any reasonable explanation?"

Out of nowhere, Alex piped up. "Yesterday it was raining," he said.

I turned on him, and even despite his puffed-up eyes, and the tears which dampened his cheeks, I couldn't prevent a touch of bile sneaking into my tone of voice. "Yeah, and I'm sure they'll *really* buy that one . . . get real, Alex, somebody *died* and we didn't inform the police because of drizzle?"

That response of mine sparked a fresh silence.

In the end it was Eric who finally chipped in.

"Whatever we decide to do, we can't stay here forever."

———

At around midmorning, and with no sign of us packing up, I set about limping around the campsite. I suppose that I was testing my ankle, seeing if it was really as shot as I imagined. Considering the pain I felt, jangling up through my entire body, the only conclusion I reached was that I should get to a hospital as soon as I possibly could. Not that the others would allow that.

It turned out to be something of a masochistic experiment, with each step I took stealing away my breath all the more. When I bumped into Mercy, on the edge of the campsite, sitting alone, her back pressed up against one of the trunks in the copse of Scots pines, the unexpected encounter seemed just as surprising for both of us.

Although Mercy was quick to press on a smile when she saw me, I didn't miss the scowl she'd been wearing before. As she'd stared into the loch with a pensive expression.

"How's the ankle?" she said, a slight hop in her voice.

. . . A *faked* hop to her voice.

"Oh, you know," I replied, "a bit sore."

"Should be back soon."

I nodded. "Hope so."

An uneasy silence settled over the two of us, and I couldn't help but be the one to break it. I had questions that I needed to have answered. "The night before last," I said, "where did you and Graeme go?"

Even as I said it an unexpected lump formed in my throat.

I swallowed it back.

Scolded myself for being a baby.

This was the Adult World now, and it was a fact of life that adults *hooked up with* other adults. I had no reason to feel like the injured party. *I* had never made a move on Graeme, and, in reality, my secret had been so well kept that Mercy had *believed* that I'd been after Alex all along.

Mercy met my eye for a second, then looked back to the loch.

To the lightly falling rain.

I was certain that she wasn't going to say anything about it, that she was going to dismiss me out of hand, but, in the end, she did open up.

"We were with you all, in the water," she said. "All of us drinking, remember?"

Although I remembered very little, I nodded along.

Not wanting to stop her flow.

"And then, it must've been close to midnight, Graeme asked if I wanted to go for a walk." Here she blushed. Her eyes averted mine. And I could tell that Mercy was somewhat nervous about relating any more of the story. But, now that she'd started, it seemed that she couldn't easily stop. "I agreed. I remember it was you, Eric, Alex and . . . and"—the name hung in her throat —"*Petra*," she finally got out. "You were all passing around a bottle of whisky, each taking nips from it on account of the cold." Mercy shook her head, smiling. "I couldn't quite believe that all of you could stand the water—*I'd* been feeling cold since a long time earlier."

"Beer jackets, I suppose."

"Hmm?" Mercy said, looking back at me. "Oh, you mean you felt warm because of the beer, and other assorted items of alcohol?"

I only smiled lightly in reply.

Often I'd noticed Mercy's slightly ditsy nature. How she seemed to slip away onto some other plane of existence at a moment of her choosing. I turned my attention back to her story. "Where did you go next?"

"Oh," Mercy said, and then reached out her arm, pointing to the slope which led up through the Scots pines . . . the slope up which Eric had got hold of the wasps nest. "We clambered up there, wanting to get some privacy." She looked back at me. "To be honest, I wasn't all that drunk, only a bit tipsy. Maybe that was why I'd been getting cold in the loch, maybe that was why it was urgent that I get out and get dry."

"I see," I replied. "And when you got up to the top of the slope?"

Mercy flushed again this time, but it was a different sort of effect. It was one of those blushes which some people of a certain age might've termed 'glowing'.

Yes, Mercy was *glowing*.

"He kissed me," she said.

I allowed myself to dwell on this fact for several moments, feeling my heart beat hard against the underside of my throat. For some reason, it felt as if that was a stolen kiss, as if *somehow* that kiss had been meant for me, and that if I'd only played my cards better . . . if only I hadn't been so *shy* . . . then it *could've* been mine. But it'd gone to Mercy.

That was the truth of the matter.

I forced myself back into the conversation, into Mercy's account. "And then you went down to the tents?"

Mercy looked me in the eye then nodded. "Yes," she said. "Don't you remember? Graeme called out over the water to you, he asked you if it was okay to take your place in the tent that night. You were all grinning, and everything, still in the water with Eric, Alex and Petra. It was funny. It felt almost as if *anything* that either of us might say to you, you would have agreed to." Mercy reached down and scratched the underside of her wrist. "I guess that just goes to show what drink does."

However, I was only half-focussed on Mercy's puritanical message because I had noticed the underside of her wrist . . . most notably the dried blood there.

Petra's blood?

Another Night On The Loch

hat night I stared into the campfire flames. We all sat on the logs we'd retrieved from nearby, on our first day at the loch. Every time that the breeze whipped in over the shore, I caught that ghastly, overwhelmingly *pungent* odour of rotting human flesh.

Of Petra's rotting flesh.

As I looked into those brilliant, orange flickers, I tried to work out just what was going on here. Just *why* we continued to stay here, at the campsite. And I had to remind myself, several times, about the dried blood I had seen on the underside of Mercy's wrist.

Could it be from anyone else other than Petra?

Noticing the dried blood had certainly got me thinking more focussedly about the others. About Graeme. I wasn't quite sure if his twitchiness, the way that at any sound—a falling branch; a *plop* of something or other falling into the loch—would make him flinch, look around, as if it had been a burst of gunfire.

Looking over Eric and Alex now, I could hardly bring to mind how I had ever suspected them. It seemed, like me, they just wanted to go home. And it appeared that it was Graeme and Mercy who were intent on staying . . . though for what purpose, I really had no idea.

Did they hope that this would all go away—that *Petra* would go away—if we only refused to move on from this spot? Or did they intend to kill the rest of us, one by one?

. . . Like they'd killed Petra . . .

There was no way of knowing.

I've never aspired to be a mind-reader.

Strangely, despite wanting more than anything to get away from the loch, and to get to the police, I found myself wondering *why* they would have done it.

I had never seen *either* of them so much as speak directly to Petra. For the most part they had used Alex as a proxy. He was a much better friend of Graeme's than Petra was.

I heard my stomach rumble and I folded in over myself, hoping to snuff out the sound.

The food had run out now, and we had nothing else to eat other than a packet of marshmallows and the last eighth of a bag of dried pasta. Graeme and Mercy had instigated the cooking of the pasta, and apportioned it out to each of us. I'd passed on the marshmallows, not really feeling capable of consuming something so sickly sweet after all that had happened. I just wanted to go home now. This crime—*whatever it was*—could wait for now.

Once 'dinner' was over and done with, I lugged myself up from the log, and made for the shore of the loch. It was then that I was surprised to find Graeme at my side, offering himself as a shoulder for me to lean my weight on. "Here," he said, "take it slow, okay?"

I realised I was shaking all over when I reached out, took a firm grip of his shoulder, and allowed my dead weight to rest on him.

Together, we headed for the shore of the loch.

"This okay here?" Graeme said, angling his head downwards to indicate a rock which stood up out of the water.

"Yeah," I said, wincing from the sudden rush of pain which passed up through my ankle.

Using those bulging—*rower's*—muscles of his, he eased me down.

I allowed my weight to pass away from him, and onto the rock below.

Just like that, I was sitting on the rock and looking out over the loch.

Rather than retreat, to retire to the tent which he and Mercy —*apparently*—shared, he crouched down beside me. He seemed to meet my gaze, and to look out over the water with me. I felt stupid—like I was his grandmother or something and that he was comforting me in my final hours of life. "I see you spoke with Mercy today."

I felt my whole body go rigid.

It took a great amount of concentrated resistance not to slip him a sidelong glance; to see if he might be carrying some sort of a weapon clutched in his fist.

"That's right," I said, my throat still dry from the few shells of pasta I'd eaten.

"She told you about what happened . . . about what happened *that night*?"

It was surprising to think that the murder had happened two nights ago now, and that, by tomorrow morning, it would be *three*.

How could that be?

How could we have left this all so long?

This time I turned and stared at Graeme directly. "She told me some things," I said, "about how you went up the slope, and then . . . back down to the tent."

I half expected to be on the end of a gloating glare, that Graeme would be showing off some sort of male pride in his latest conquest. However, there was nothing of *pride* there at all.

It surprised me all the more when he reached out for my hand, curled my limp fingers about his own. Then he stared back into my eyes. "I've always thought, you know, Charlie, that you and I would be good together."

My heart beat against my ribs.

I didn't understand what he was saying.

Couldn't understand what he was saying.

But even if I'd wanted to run it would've been impossible . . . not with my ankle . . . not with *nowhere* to run to. No weapon.

"It's funny the way things work out, huh?" he said, breaking off our gaze, and looking back out over the water. "It's just, that night, you know, it felt *right*."

Although I was certain I'd heard *that* particular line spoken by the love rat in just about every single daytime film I'd ever suffered through, I couldn't *help* myself.

I couldn't shut down those most *stupid* of female urges.

My feminine *pride*.

He squeezed my hand tighter.

And I decided that now was the time to spill my concerns.

"I saw the blood, Graeme, on Mercy's wrist."

I studied Graeme's reaction, hoping to catch him flinching.

But he hardly moved at all.

He didn't release my hand.

Then, finally, he looked back at me. "Did you ask her where it came from?"

I shook my head.

He nodded to himself, as if he was understanding some deep, dark secret which I—poor little *naïve* girl that I was—would never understand.

Not even in a hundred lifetimes.

"When she went to see the body," Graeme said, "when you and Eric *came across* the body, she couldn't help herself. She wanted to know for sure. She wanted to know that the blood was *real*." He stared back into my eyes, his lips pressed tightly together. "It was a stupid thing to do, sure, but she did it. She reached out and *touched* the wound." He shook his head. "She did the best she could to get the blood off afterwards in the loch, but there's only so much you can do with cold water . . . it should be gone in a few days, but don't you see?" He squeezed my hand all the more intently. "We can't go to the police, they'll bring out their forensic scientists, they'll *know* Mercy touched the body. They'll think that *she* did it."

I realised, when I glanced back over my shoulder, that the campfire had crackled down into nothing at all. That the others had retreated to their tents. I wondered if they could overhear our conversation, if they'd been hanging on every word.

In the end, I couldn't help asking the question. "Did she do it?"

———

Despite feeling completely worn out, I knew that there was little hope for me in terms of getting some sleep. I was simply too worked up by all that had gone on.

That night, I didn't even bother to go into the tent which I would share with Eric and Alex. I decided to stay on that rock, staring out over the water.

Even as I stared into the unfurling darkness, I couldn't shift that expression of Graeme's; that look of . . . of *disappointment* which'd struck his features.

As if he was *disappointed* in me for thinking such a thing about Mercy.

That she might be capable of such a thing.

The truth was, though, I didn't really know Mercy all that well.

I didn't really know *any* of them all that well.

Who were these people?

And what had they done to Petra?

I must've been sitting on the rock for hours and hours, looking out over the water, before I convinced myself to get up; to use the walking pole which Eric had crafted for himself.

A little time after Graeme had slipped off to bed, Eric had come out of the tent to hand me the pole in some apparent fit of altruism.

I used it to help myself up onto my good leg, and then made my way steadily across the shore of the loch, towards the copse of Scots pines, and the pathway which led up and away from our campsite. It took the best part of twenty minutes to get up to the top of the slope so that I could look down on the loch; on the campsite.

It was hard to believe, in the beautiful, streaming moonlight, that this scenery could've been the setting for such a barbaric act of cruelty.

As I leaned up against the cane, I could feel the sweat drooling down the sides of my face. My heart was beating hard. I knew it would be a real challenge to make it back along the trail unaided.

But, in any case, I turned to look.

Saw the beaten-in path we'd travelled to the loch along.

Would it really be so tough?

With all of the others sleeping now, all of them out for the night, could I make it back to the village before daybreak . . . before they even woke up?

I thought about what the others had said; about how we needed to stick together.

And it was then that the plan—*their plan*—struck me.

Whoever had been responsible, they were being protected by the others. It would take me until at least daybreak before I reached the village, and, when I did, I could almost guarantee that at least one of them would've already stirred; noticed I wasn't there. They would rouse the others and, together, they'd set about conjuring some story which would implicate me.

It would become a case of 'he said, she said' . . .

They would—*all of them*—stand against me.

I thought the matter through some more. It would take the police's forensic scientists to absolve me from any kind of misdoing in the murder . . . and could I *really* trust that they'd come out with the right answer, that they *wouldn't* brand the crime scene as being 'contaminated' ?

Although I was intent on doing the right thing, I realised— right then—that it was contingent on me putting my own neck on the line. I wanted to make myself safe before I went and did anything rash. Something which would turn the others away from me forever.

Maybe I stood up on the hillside for longer than an hour, staring along the path, mentally mapping my route back to the village, and, with each heartbeat, telling myself that I needed to go *now*. But I held myself still. Rooted to the spot. Leaning against the walking pole.

I knew I couldn't do it.

That I had to think things through better.

As I turned my back on the pathway, I felt the toe of my boot come into heavy contact with an object in the long grass. I paused, bent down, using the walking pole to help keep the weight off my ankle, and I scooped it up.

My pocket knife.

I looked it over—its sleek, burgundy casing.

I flipped out a few of the implements, observed the moon-light sheen across the sharpened edges. As I replaced the knife in my pocket, I thought about how, if the others had *really* wanted to incriminate me, then they would've done well to connect my knife, in some way, with the murder.

But they *hadn't* thought it out.

No.

Whoever was responsible for Petra's death, they hadn't thought things out *at all*.

And that made me wonder if it had been a crime committed in the heat of the moment. Surely all murders follow a similar pattern. Adrenalin. Lack of thought.

Knowing there was nothing else I could do, I set off again, back towards the shore of the loch; already wondering what new horrors the next day would bring.

———

I woke with a start sometime around dawn.

At first, I thought it was either Eric or Alex, talking in their sleep, or perhaps jerking their limbs. But, when I lifted myself up —feeling that now-familiar jangle of pain through my ankle—I saw that both Alex and Eric were sleeping soundly.

I picked my way carefully over their sleeping bodies, not wanting to stir either one. It was a harder task to unzip the tent flap silently, but, for the most part, I managed it.

As the cool morning breeze caught my cheeks, I inadvertently brushed the plastic bag which contained the 'empties' from our blow-out on that fateful night. The tin cans within jangled a little, and I heard a pair of glass bottles *clink* together.

I made it out of the tent, zipping the flap back up, without waking either Eric or Alex.

Outside, on the campsite, I held myself very still, listening for the sound which'd woken me. It took a fair few seconds before I heard it again.

Sure.

Obvious.

And close.

Footsteps.

I jerked my head around.

Strained my eyes to see what I might be able to see.

As I did, I saw the figure, on the opposite bank of the loch.

He wore a black plastic rain cape—or perhaps it was a dustbin liner—and he was clambering his way up the slope. He had a beige—hemp?—bag hoisted over his shoulder. As he strode, his gait seemed to become larger, more determined, as the gradient of the hill increased. He seemed to be in some sort of a hurry . . . and at this *early* hour. And in the middle of nowhere.

I grabbed my walking pole, which I'd left leaning up against the side of the tent, and I made my way—slowly—about the periphery of the loch.

It was day by the time I got around to the point where I'd seen the man.

He had ended up here, somewhere close.

Wherever his destination happened to be.

I took care with the many rabbit holes scattered about under-foot, not wanting to turn the other ankle. It took me maybe twice as long to get to the top of the hill as normal.

But I got there.

I peered over the sight, immediately seeing the man in the plastic rain cape from earlier. At close quarters, I could clearly tell that it *was* a dustbin liner.

He had wispy, white hair which clung onto his reddened, nearly bald scalp. His cheeks, and his whole complexion, were a pinkish red. I wondered if he had any family—if they knew that he was up here. That he was all alone and, at least to my eye, clearly in need of help. That said, I saw that he was sat slumped on the flattened long grasses with something in his lap. I soon realised it was a rabbit. It had greeny-grey fur and white splodges all over its body. The way the rabbit lay on the man's lap, with its head at an odd angle, told me that it wasn't a *living* rabbit any longer.

That this was the man's breakfast.

Well, at least the man didn't seem to have issues finding food.

As if anticipating my thoughts, the man tilted his head and squinted at me.

I realised that the sun was rising right behind my head. I shifted a little so that he could get a better look at who he was talking to.

Apparently having seen whatever he was looking for, he turned his head back down to his rabbit. I saw that he'd produced a knife from somewhere and was setting about cutting into its skin. Ready to peel it back, to do whatever he needed to do to make it edible.

"Lovely girl," I heard him mumble under his breath.

"Excuse me?" I said, leaning on my cane.

He chuckled to himself and shook his head. ". . . Lovely girl."

I wondered if he was referring to the rabbit, or to me.

I suppose it could've been either.

Or both.

Searching for conversation, I finally got out, "Nice morning, isn't it?"

Not looking up from the rabbit the man replied, " 'Nice morning', yes 'tis."

I looked down, out over the loch. I could see the tents clearly from there, of course. There was no sign of anybody stirring yet. My eyes lingered, for the longest time, on the brown tent.

The one in which Petra's body lay.

I turned back to the man. "Do you often come up here?"

" 'Up here' ?" the man said, busy skinning the rabbit. "Yes —*up here.*"

"I wanted to ask if you'd, uh, maybe, a few nights ago . . ."

But the man started into jabbering something to himself. His chuntering words seemed to work as a kind of accompaniment for his sawing at the rabbit's hide.

Despite never having really been all that keen about eating freshly hunted animals, I couldn't help but feel a slight *thrum* of hunger pass through my stomach. It had been a few days since I'd eaten anything substantial . . . I didn't feel much in the mood to eat around the others. There was something about openly held suspicion which worked on me like a dietary suppressant.

Faintly, I hoped the man might offer me a little slice of his rabbit.

When he was done *cooking* it, of course.

"You see," I went on, and then, realising that the man clearly wasn't in his right mind, I'd have to be very clear—speak in plain terms—I said, "There was a *murder*, down at the campsite." I reached out and pointed back to the tents on the opposite shore. "Down there."

The man paused for a second, glanced up at me, then looked to my finger.

To where I pointed.

He seemed to take in what I was communicating.

" 'Murder' ?" he repeated back at me.

"Uh-huh," I replied, and, at the same time, realised just how ridiculous it sounded to be blasé about the whole thing. "*Murder.*"

The man seemed to look inside himself, the rabbit spread across his lap forgotten for the time being. He jawed silently, as if he was articulating his thoughts out loud, but so that he would be the only one to hear.

"I was wondering if you, uh"—the craziness of the whole situation sunk in with me for several seconds and I didn't know if I could go on; but I forced myself—"did you *see* anything? It would've been night-time. A few weeks ago . . . a *hatchet*," I added, at the same time mimicking a chopping motion.

" 'Hatchet,' " the man said back to me. " 'A hatchet'."

My heart hung in my throat for several moments, just to think that I'd shared what'd gone on back at the campsite with someone else. That I'd broken the *omertà*, or whatever..

The man made the motion of chopping back at me, his watery green eyes meeting mine.

Down, at the campsite, I noticed some movement.

One of the tents zipping open.

I saw that it was Eric's tent . . . that Alex was sticking his head out.

There wasn't much time.

What I was doing here was suspicious.

And it wouldn't help any of them—*at all*—to 'trust' me.

I turned back to the man dressed in the bin liner. "They *killed* her. With the hatchet. Did you see anything? Did you see anyone with the hatchet?"

But the man simply turned back to me.

His expression blank.

And he said, " 'Hatchet' ?"

I realised then that I'd lost him, so I thanked him for the little help he'd been able to give me and turned back to the campsite.

A Plan

"Who's that?" Alex said, as I returned to the camp, limping my way across the pebbled shore, feeling the ache of my ankle working its way up the back of my leg.

Alex was looking out across the loch, of course, to the man in the bin liner who I'd been speaking to. When I followed his gaze, I saw that the man had brought a fire blazing out of the ground. I imagined that he'd already started into cooking that rabbit of his.

I suppose, without me to distract him, the task was a much swifter one.

Black smoke billowed up into the morning air. It floated away from where we were camped on the shore so there wasn't even the prospect of getting so much as a *whiff* of the cooking rabbit.

Of cooking *meat*.

"Just some wanderer," I finally replied, to Alex.

I judged Alex's expression for a long while, saw his latched-jaw look.

"I'd be careful with that open mouth, you'll catch flies."

As if in acknowledgement of this quip—if it could even be called that—he shut his mouth tight, and turned his attention back to the tents behind us.

When I returned to Eric's tent, I saw that he was curled around himself in his sleeping bag. Apparently unaware of all that was going on around us . . . of the dreadful situation which we found ourselves in.

I coughed loudly.

Still sleeping, Eric frowned, and then he blinked a couple of times. Finally, he wrenched an eye open and looked out at me. "Yeah?" he said.

"Are we leaving today?" I asked. "Are we going to the police?"

Eric blinked several times again, and I wondered if he truly had forgotten why we were still here, on Loch Monar. But, when he reached up and rubbed his temple a few times, he seemed to regain some sort of awareness. "Going?" he said.

"Yes, you know, finally *leaving* the loch . . . telling them what happened to Petra?"

Eric remained stunned for a few moments, and I wondered if he'd been drinking the night before. He had that sort of grim, brought-back-to-life quality to him. "We . . . we'll have to ask Graeme."

So there was the confirmation that Graeme—after all this—was the one in charge of the whole *wanting-to-stay-behind* business.

I shifted away from Eric, leaving him to doze away some more.

When I emerged in the sunlight, seeing Alex still sitting out on the shore of the loch, looking thoroughly lost, I noticed that Graeme was already up and out of his tent. He eyed me closely, slipped me a smile. But his charm wasn't going to work for him this time.

In fact, I was determined that it wasn't going to work for him ever again.

. . . At least not on me.

I felt like some kind of a crone supporting myself with the cane and limping my way towards him. "You killed her, didn't you?" I said, surprising even myself at the bite in my words.

I half expected Graeme to get all defensive, to suddenly begin denying it, like suspects do in films. But, instead, he simply smiled wider. "You've got it all sussed out, haven't you?"

Right then, I couldn't quite believe that I'd *ever* thought him to possess any sort of grace or charm. At the moment, he just seemed to be a colossal idiot.

"Why don't you want to go to the police?"

"I want justice," he replied, backing away from the tent, inside of which I supposed Mercy was still sleeping away.

"The police will give us justice."

"Not if we don't play our cards right."

I shook my head. "Why're you so afraid of going to the police? What *is* it that you're so worried about? What do you have to *hide*?"

Graeme's smile dialled down a couple of notches. He met my eye with a firmer gaze now. "I had an uncle once," Graeme said. "Got himself into a situation similar to this one. Been out drinking with some of his buddies in the local pub. Next thing he noticed, one of his buddies had slipped off. All the others assumed that he'd just gone off to the toilets, that he'd be back soon, but he was gone such a long time that my uncle thought that he should go take a look for him.

"When my uncle came across him, in a back alley, he'd been bludgeoned to death. Blood everywhere. Up the walls. Puddles of it on the ground. My uncle went to the police and he'd still be in prison till this day if he hadn't hung himself a year ago."

I felt a chill pass through my chest.

My heart rapped my ribs.

But I still managed to keep my thoughts straight.

To deal them to Graeme in a logical order.

"And what about if your uncle was guilty—what about if he was *drunk* and didn't remember doing his friend in?"

Graeme moved quickly, straight off the spot. I guess that him and his rowing pals had all done a good amount of sprint training to get in shape for races. He grabbed me about the throat, and I felt his muscular fingers sink into my skin. With his body close to mine, I smelled the sweet-sour scent of sex clinging to him.

I could hardly breathe.

Graeme tightened his grip.

Lifted me up off the ground.

The pain about my throat was almost too much to bear.

"You listen, and you listen *now*, all right?" Graeme said. "Nobody says a *fucking* thing about my family and gets away with it, 'kay?"

I tried to respond but I couldn't manage to get the air in the right places.

"*Graeme!*" Mercy called out from somewhere behind us.

Graeme half turned, looked to her, the same expression of absolute rage consuming his features. He seemed to realise where he was—what he was doing. I felt his grip ease off my throat, and, slowly, I descended to the ground.

When both my feet met with the firm rocky floor, I forgot all about my ankle. The pain which twisted about the joint was nothing compared with the pumping welts at my throat, from where Graeme had held me with his firm-fingered grip.

Before that moment no man had ever put his hands on me like that. No man had ever carried out a *physical* attack on me . . .

I wasn't sure how to feel. If I should feel somehow violated, or *wronged* . . . had I done anything to provoke Graeme, beyond pointing out the obviousness of the similarities between our situations? I didn't think so.

But, then again, sometimes it's difficult to judge my own tone of voice; the spirit with which I say things. Maybe I'd done something else to rile Graeme . . . perhaps I'd given him the strongest hint of the truth which none of us dared speak; that the murderer *was* among us.

And that nobody wanted to fess up.

A drunken night wasn't enough to lose memories.

Not in my opinion.

With that thought on my mind, I was certain there was something I wasn't seeing . . . something which was staring me right in the face.

Why wouldn't I allow myself to see it?

———

Later on that day, I lay in the tent beside Eric.

It seemed that Eric was stuck in the same funk from earlier; his brain elsewhere. He stared up at the ceiling of the tent as if there was some movie being projected onto it.

Outside, I could hear yet more mumbling, between Alex, and Graeme, and—among that sound—I heard the scratching and cobbling-together of the tent alongside us.

It seemed that—*finally*—Graeme had snapped to his senses.

That we were going to allow the authorities to take it from here.

To determine who among us was the murderer.

It surprised me when Eric broke the silence in the tent.

When he spoke to me.

"That night," he said, "I remembered something about it . . . about being in the water."

"What about being in the water?"

"You know," Eric went on, his voice slightly floaty, almost otherworldly, "when we were all swimming about, in the loch. All of us. We were all drinking."

I turned my own mind back, thinking of the numbing water. About how I had had that pleasant warming sensation right down in my gut from the alcohol. From the whisky, rum . . . and whatever else was being passed around.

Eric continued, "While we were swimming about, or whatever, I remember holding onto that bottle of vodka"—right, there had been vodka, too—"and, for the first time, Petra spoke up. She'd been quiet almost all day. I think everyone was surprised to hear her say anything at all. It was when Graeme said something about getting home, about wanting to be with his dogs, and his sheep . . . his *cows* . . . you know, whatever the hell else his family has on that farm of his."

I chuckled under my breath, glad for being able to laugh about Graeme. He certainly did have certain cartoonish elements to him, and, I think, my attraction towards him often blinded me to those qualities.

Eric went on, "Well, I remember Petra speaking up, saying how she'd thought she'd smelled some manure while we'd been about the loch that week; and yet there'd been no farm animals in sight. She said that the mystery had been solved."

I felt my chest tighten.

Already, I drew comparisons with the event which I'd experienced just now.

With Graeme flipping out on me, grabbing me by the throat and hoisting me upwards.

Eric shook his head. "It wasn't anything really, just a look, but

I couldn't remember seeing Graeme look that way before . . . it seemed as if, I dunno . . ."

"As if he could kill?"

Eric turned his head to mine, met my eye.

He pressed his lips firmly together.

Then gave a solemn nod.

————

Even despite my ankle injury, I did far more for our packing-up efforts than Eric, who continued to just sort of *float* along in his own little world. What he might've been thinking, was anybody's guess. Although I did my best to stay out of Graeme's way as he packed up Mercy's tent, there did come a time when, standing side by side, each of us preparing our rucksacks, we were alone together. I noticed that Graeme was staring at me intently, giving me a sidelong glance. I looked back to him. "What?" I said. "Are you going to flip out on me again?"

"I wanted to apologise," Graeme said. "What happened . . . you know, it's not *me*."

The only thing which I could bring to mind to say back to him was, *Well, if it wasn't* you *then just who was it?* . . . but I restrained myself.

It wouldn't do any good to trample over a peace offering when it was on the table.

He held out his hand to me.

I shook it.

His skin felt cold, and slippery, like *fish* scales.

He withdrew his hand as soon as he possibly could.

Then, using the same hand, he combed his fingers through his hair. "It's just this whole situation, you know, just everything that's gone on. It's got me under stress."

78

I wondered to myself how someone could be so self-absorbed, but, at the same time, reminded myself of how most of the murderers I'd seen on TV, in films, believed the world revolved around them. How might Graeme have felt if he'd been held prisoner by those who he had considered 'friends' ? I waited for a while before attempting anything like a probing tone to my voice.

"So," I said, "have you got the story all worked out now?"

Maybe I expected Graeme to fly into pure rage again, to grab hold of me, to smash my head against the rocks. Instead, he flashed me a smile. There was something measured about him, almost contrived . . . as if he had made a deal with himself not to show his hand any longer.

And if that meant him not trying to strangle me then I couldn't say I was all that upset.

"I think we've got things settled," Graeme replied, and then jerked his head off to the hillside opposite, where I could still see a few strands of smoke from a dying fire rising up into the sky. "That drifter—he'll get the blame. Everyone goes home happy."

Graeme reached down for his rucksack, snapped something into place, and then ripped open one of the zip-up pockets.

I stared off across the loch, thought about the man from that morning, and the rabbit he'd had spread across his lap. Beside everything, beside the fact that the man had seemed to be somewhat disconnected from reality, I wasn't certain that the story would wash.

Such a brutal murder . . . and from someone who seemed so innocent . . .

As Graeme hoisted his rucksack up over his shoulder, looked back over the campsite to the others—all of them ready to go too —I couldn't help but speak up. "Look," I said, "I don't understand. If one of us killed Petra then they should come forward.

It's not right to do this. Not right at all. Why're we trying to cover things up?"

A stony silence descended over the group.

I looked, in turn, to each and every person's face, hoping that I might be able to find an ally somewhere, but, of course, nobody seemed capable of standing up to Graeme . . . nobody wanted to fight at my side when Graeme was on the other. Finally, because I'd gone that far, I thought to add a little more. "Who killed Petra? Come forward now, it's the only way. Why're you hiding?"

Again, I looked about their faces, trying to meet my 'friends' eyes, and finding it next to impossible. Why *was* this all such a secret? Why was *I* the only one who was left out of the loop?

As if I hadn't said anything at all, Graeme cut in. "Someone needs to stay behind, with the body, so that nobody tampers with the scene." He pointed off across the loch, to the dwindling smoke on the hillside. "And to keep an eye on the drifter, to see he doesn't get too far . . . it'd be a tricky thing if we lose track of him."

My chest tightened.

I felt a pang of pain pass through my ankle.

Before I could say anything, Eric chipped in. "I'll stay," he said, slipping his rucksack down off his shoulder. Laying it at his feet.

"Me too," I said.

Graeme looked between me and Eric, flashed us a smile, and then, with the sleeveless shirt exposing his rippling biceps, he set off along the path. Headed back to civilisation.

Mercy following in his footsteps.

Alex lagged behind them, looked to me briefly, and then said, in a cramped voice, "I'm going to stay behind too—to be with her."

Graeme turned back for a fraction of a second, cast his eye

over Alex—it seemed as if there was some kind of disapproval there, but I couldn't be certain. In any case, Graeme stiffly nodded, and then set off along the path, headed away from the campsite.

Leaving the three of us behind.

Mercy held back a moment, and then, with an apologetic smile, slipped the rolled-up tent off the top of her rucksack, and handed it to me. "Won't do us much use," she said, "you'll be better off with it, I suspect."

I mouthed a word of thanks as she and Graeme headed off along the path.

We watched Graeme and Mercy slip from sight, disappearing among the Scots pines, and head away from the campsite.

"Well," Eric said, his voice a little lighter, almost *jovial*. "Maybe we should put that fishing rod of mine to use, eh? Might get some dinner so we don't starve to death."

Fishing At Sunset

I *crouched* on the shore feeling my tender ankle twisting beneath my weight. I would've done just about anything for some kind of a painkiller, but us being the proverbial amateur campers, not one of us had thought to pack any.

The sun set behind the hills on the opposite side of the loch. I supposed I must've been tired, ready to turn in and go to sleep, but the truth was that I felt more weary than anything else. I just wanted this all to be over. I wanted to return to Inverness . . . be done with all this strangeness.

Be done with all this deception.

I observed Eric with the fishing rod, slumped over himself on a rock. He hardly had the strength to hold the rod straight anymore. He only exerted the very minimum of energy to keep the rod above the surface of the water. A couple of times there had been twitches on the surface, fish waggling up, nibbling at something or other, generally not bothering to give the hook more than a passing glance. To tell the truth, I wasn't all that hungry, so although I guessed I should've felt somewhat more anxious about Eric catching our dinner, I just couldn't muster the motivation.

Alex stood at the opposite end of the shore, his gaze also fixed on Eric's fishing line, and where it entered the water. It was anybody's guess what he might've been thinking.

About Petra?

. . . About *Graeme*?

About whoever it was who had killed her?

I was certain that they all knew the answer.

But they wouldn't tell me.

Why?

When the voice sounded behind me, I flinched, turned sharply.

Saw that it was the man from before.

The one who I'd met on the other side of the loch.

The drifter.

He wore the same rain cape I'd seen him in previously, and his hair looked a touch damp as if he had recently taken a wash in the loch. He tilted his head to one side then said, "Can teach . . . *you*."

Only when he raised his arm, pointing with his gnarled, yellow-brown fingernails, did I realise he was indicating Eric who was still trying—*and failing*—to catch our dinner.

I turned my attention back to the drifter. "Uh, okay," I replied.

But the drifter, apparently not bothering to await my opinion, was already striding his way to the shore. He stood over Eric for several minutes.

Eric finally realised the drifter was standing behind him thanks to a nod from Alex.

I couldn't resist the sneaky smile which peeled back the corners of my mouth. Just as I had done, Eric flinched to turn around and notice the drifter standing there.

I heard the drifter's voice—muffled, almost unintelligible—as he mumbled out the same thing which he had said to me . . . about wanting to help us out.

I shifted a glance over to Alex, who had pulled the hood of his sweatshirt up so that it obscured his face. He looked away from me quickly, and I turned back to the interaction playing out between Eric and the drifter.

Eric gave up the fishing rod willingly, apparently pleased to defer the task to someone else. The drifter took the rod from him, and then, crouching down in a position which mimicked how Eric had previously been, he reeled in the line before casting it out again with a sharp flick of his wrist.

I watched on as the float splashed into the surface of the loch, sending ripples cresting in neat concentric circles.

For the longest time, all of us remained there, on the shore of the loch.

I listened to the birdsong, to the *chitter* and *chatter* of the birds as they readied for bed. I wondered if there weren't a few piercing whistles from bats as they bombed back and forth, gathering the bugs which fluttered dozily in the peach-toned sunset.

All of us were quite still.

I only noticed how cold it had got, and that the sun had slunk beneath the horizon, when I wrapped my arms about myself and felt goose pimples rising up out of my flesh.

The drifter was completely still. He was bowed down low as if he was a human being from some distinct time or place. Somewhere *much* simpler, much more *basic* . . . as if he could hear the tremors and trundles of the Earth as easily as his own heartbeat.

And then, without warning, the drifter snapped upright.

He reeled the fishing rod swiftly.

Yanked it back from the surface of the loch.

I watched on as the form of the fish flapped and flailed as it was pulled from the water.

Neatly—*quickly*—the drifter pivoted around.

He allowed the fish to come to rest on the shore.

Then placed the fishing rod down gently on the pebbles.

The way he snuck up to the fish, a hefty rock clutched in his fist, reminded me again of some hunter-gatherer. Someone more elemental. Impossibly in touch with his surroundings.

As if he was a conductor finishing off the brutal refrain of a symphony, he brought the rock down. Again and again. Renewed fury each time. Striking the fish until it no longer moved.

Until it was dead.

And, as the drifter leaned back from his kill, I couldn't help but picture Petra in my mind.

Think about whether or not this scene might've mimicked the one which'd played out in the past. And which one of my 'friends' had played the role of the drifter.

The one who had delivered the coup de grâce.

———

I breathed in the gentle scent of smoke and cooking fish.

The campfire crackled away before us . . . before me, and Eric, and the drifter.

Alex stood a little way away.

Still staring out over the loch.

Perhaps he was examining the play of the flames in the water's reflection.

I chewed through what remained of my fish—*a trout*—and eyed the other eight which lay on a nearby flat stone, ready to be cooked and eaten. The drifter clearly had a knack for catching fish; as if he possessed some higher relationship with nature, with our surroundings.

Something which none of us would ever be able to completely comprehend.

After the first fish, he had yanked them out, one after the other, in a successive chain.

As he had pulled them free of the water, I helped to collect them up, to lay them down on the flat stone for cooking later. And I couldn't help but notice the drifter's expression. How his face betrayed neither pleasure or satisfaction. He remained neutral the entire time, as if this was nothing but a normal day's work for him . . . then again, considering how much I knew about him—considering how much *we* knew about him—it might well have been.

Hadn't I seen him skinning a rabbit earlier?

Once we'd finished with our dinner, we all sat around and stared into the campfire.

Even Alex tired of staring into the loch endlessly, lost to his own thoughts. He eventually came over to join us. Even eating one of the fish for himself.

I half expected the drifter to leave us once we had finished with our eating, but, it seemed, he had decided to stay with us.

The wind had picked up a little, and a gentle, misty drizzle was falling.

It rattled slightly coming into contact with the drifter's rain cape.

And didn't at all affect his hardened expression as he stared into the campfire.

When I finally glanced up, I saw that Eric and Alex were

both staring at me, waiting to see what I would do next, as if —*somehow*—this drifter had suddenly become *my* responsibility.

I decided that we did need to say something . . . to *talk*.

"So," I said, breaking the silence, and vaguely directing my words to the drifter, "have you been living around here for a long time?"

The drifter continued to stare into the flames, apparently unmoved by my words. When I breathed in, I caught the thick, oily scent of fish. And a little of the drifter's musk.

Living out in nature certainly did little for personal hygiene.

I guessed that all of us could do with a hot shower and a thorough soaping.

Right when I'd believed the drifter to have forgotten all about us—to have slipped away into whichever portion of his mind he resided in—he straightened up.

Looked me in the eye.

His pupils seemed inky—*black*—in the darkness.

" . . . 'A long time' . . ." the drifter replied.

I was unsure whether this was his answer, or if he was merely repeating one of the phrases which I had spoken to him. Before I had the chance to confirm, the drifter rose. Arched his shoulders back. Glanced about our camp, and then, without reason or explanation, he strode off in the opposite direction from the one where he'd arrived.

I looked to Alex, and then Eric.

"Seems a little unhinged," Eric said.

Although I couldn't see his face, I guessed, from his tone of voice, that he was smiling wryly.

"He's perfect," Alex put in.

I shook my head. " 'Perfect' for what?"

"As the prime suspect," Alex said.

I stared down into the flames, watching as they danced across the grey bark of the logs stacked up before us. "I don't under-stand," I said. "I don't understand what's going on . . . why neither of you—why *none* of you will let me know what's going on."

"It's better you know nothing," Eric finally added.

I looked to him, feeling that this was the first time he had come close to giving anything substantial away about Petra's murder. "Why is it better?" I said. "It's not like it'll make *me* guilty, now, is it?"

Eric shrugged. "It might—it might *not*."

I felt a rage twist my gut.

My blood ran impossibly hot.

I couldn't hold myself back any longer.

I launched myself up onto my feet, stamped past the fire and grabbed hold of the collar of Eric's t-shirt. I waited for Alex to come to Eric's rescue, and told myself to be ready when he did. But he seemed to see sense. To remain seated on the log surrounding the campfire.

I stared into Eric's eyes.

No sign of his smile now.

Neither did he struggle against my hold.

"What's going *on*?" I said.

"You don't remember, do you?" Eric said, his voice clearly stifled because of how I was restricting the flow of air through his throat.

"I'm *sick* of remembering—or *not* remembering, okay? Can we just agree that all of us were drunk that night. That *none* of us have a crystal-clear recollection of what went on?"

Eric did now attempt to worm free of my grasp.

But I held tight to him.

Giving him just enough slack so that he could get out a few choice words.

He gave up his struggle, met my eye again, and said, "You don't remember what you *said*, do you?"

I felt my chest tighten. A fresh warmth ploughed through my veins. "What did I say?"

Eric stared back into my eyes for the longest time, before breaking off the glare and turning his attention over to Alex. When Eric spoke again, he sounded calmer, his voice cleaner —*crisper* . . . and I knew, if nothing else, I was going to get the truth.

"We were all in the water, in the *loch*"—he jerked his head in the direction of the water as if I might've clean forgotten where we were—"all of us were drinking, you know, chatting about this and that. You and Petra, you two were standing next to one another, in the water, both of you with your beers . . . I think there was a bottle of rum, or something, too. You were watching me and Alex racing . . . remember?"

I cast my mind back, feeling that night wrapping itself around me like a damp blanket.

I could hear those splashes.

The kicking of feet.

The thrashing of arms.

As they sped away from me . . . further out onto the loch . . . further into the darkness.

Soon, I had lost sight of them.

Me *and* Petra had lost sight of them.

I could still remember the stillness, and the silence, between us.

Neither of us had anything in common.

We were only drawn together because of logistics.

Because Petra's boyfriend was part of our geography group.

I could just about recall attempting to make conversation, asking Petra what she studied. She had been elusive for a long time; never really speaking to any of us. It was as I heard the other two closing in, returning from their swim, that she turned to me and told me that she studied Russian Literature. I had no idea what to say to that.

And—

"You remember, don't you?" Eric said, cutting through my reminiscing. "You remember what you said to her . . . both of us"—Eric flashed a gesture at Alex and then back at himself as if to emphasise the point—"we *heard* what you said."

This time it was Alex who spoke up, in a cool, measured voice. "You said that Russian Literature sounded like a 'waste of time'. She was delicate," Alex said. "You weren't to know, but that's the truth of it. Everything was going against her . . . back home, her mother was ill . . . her father died about a year before. One of her sisters got hit by a lorry, ended up in a wheelchair." He stared down at his feet. "It wasn't a sure thing that she would ever be able to finish her course here, although I wanted, more than anything, for her to stay."

I shook my head, unable to quite believe the direction this conversation was headed.

"Anything might've set her off, you know?" Alex continued, looking back up at me. "What me and Eric heard—what you said —might've been enough."

"Enough for *what*?" I said.

Over the flames of the campfire, Alex met my eyes, slowly, carefully. "Enough so that she might've killed herself."

For several moments, I was simply lost by this rapid shift in the course of events.

I couldn't quite grasp it.

I felt distant from the scene, from the two of them. I let go of Eric . . . perhaps it was a subconscious reaction . . . unable to fully focus my attention on restraining him any longer.

In The Day, Darkness

My resources being used for other reasons.
And because I knew that that wasn't what I'd said at all.
What I'd said to her had been worse.
Much worse.
Now I remembered . . .

Remembering

W*e had been in the water*, that much was true. And I could recall Alex and Eric approaching, having finished that swimming race they had felt compelled to participate in. And I could remember expressing my opinion, telling Petra that I thought her course was a waste of time . . . but they hadn't heard what had come before.

They hadn't heard what she'd said to me while they'd been out of earshot.

Going about their boy games.

Swimming out into the loch.

Pumped with alcohol.

Petra had confided in me . . . not *everything*, but enough . . . I supposed that she didn't have someone she could talk to—that she could *really* talk to . . . someone who wasn't Alex.

She told me she felt worthless, and that she wanted to find a way out of her situation, but she couldn't see one. She had asked me whether or not I had ever considered suicide. I had told her yes, I had. And then she'd asked if I regretted not having gone through with it.

In retrospect, I realised what a monster I must've appeared.

But, at the same time, I wasn't exactly in any sort of a solid mental state, given that I'd drunk my weight in alcohol, and that the object of my lust—*Graeme*—had just slipped off with another girl. I wasn't in any sort of a place to be offering advice . . .

So I had given the only advice that'd come to mind.

I'd told her that *not* killing myself had been the biggest mistake of my life.

But I was certain—from the way I'd phrased it—I'd spoken in jest.

Was it because Petra spoke English as a second language that she might not have caught onto my subtle, sarcastic tone? . . . No, Petra's English had been excellent . . . and that just made me wonder if—*perhaps*—she was searching for some kind of signal, some kind of sign, from someplace.

And I had provided it.

I turned my attention back to Eric, and to Alex. "You mean, you think that she might've killed herself, with that hatchet? Chopped at her own throat?"

The two of them stared back at me.

I shook my head, still disbelieving. "And you didn't think to fill me in on this . . . all of you have been *conspiring* to create some sort of plot—a *story*—around this situation, because . . . ?"

The silence spoke volumes.

So, there it was, finally we'd found the killer.

The one responsible for *murdering* Petra . . . at least in a round-about way . . .

But was it really that simple?

"Look," I said, "I still don't get this, not at all, if you believe that it was suicide, that Petra did this herself, then why all the mystery? . . . Why was Graeme acting the way he was?"

"Because," Eric said, "without a killer, without a motive, there'll always be a mystery. Haven't you ever read about *those kids* who have a friend among them turn up dead?"

Once more, I couldn't help but feel appalled at the way in which Petra's death was being handled . . . that she'd been relegated to little more than an inconvenience.

"And, yeah," Eric went on, "maybe they *are* all truly innocent, but that doesn't do anything to ward off the suspicion . . . there'll always be those who *talk* . . . who believe that they *did* have something to do with the death."

"So," I said, looking from Eric to Alex, "you were all trying to cover your backs?"

Again, the silence spoke for them.

Finally, Alex met my eye and said, "You have to understand that we were covering *your* back too. We don't want *any* of us to have any trouble over this—we're *all* innocent."

"And because of that, we should accuse that drifter—the guy who caught our dinner?"

Again, nothing from Alex or Eric.

"Why?" I said. "Because he won't notice . . . because it'll all be the same to him? That he'll be as crazy out here as in some padded cell?"

I heard my own words echoing off across the loch.

I wondered if the drifter might be listening into our conversation.

Able to understand far more than we gave him credit for.

"Listen," Eric said, "we knew you'd have issues with this, Charlie, but this is what we've decided, okay? This is how things have to be." He flashed a glance to Alex. "We had to get things straight before we went to the police."

I thought about this again, and then thought of how I'd only been let into the big picture—into the *plan*—at this late juncture. And that was when it struck me.

I turned on Eric and Alex, said, "You were planning on handing me in, weren't you? Telling the police that *I* was responsible?"

. . . Suddenly I could see why Eric and Alex were clearly so uneager about facing up to a police interview. The two of them would simply sit there and say nothing at all.

Merely confirming their guilt.

———

Time, out in the wilderness, shifts completely. The entire frame of its meaning transforms.

Whereas, back in civilisation—back with *electricity*—I would often stay up until the early hours of the morning; on the internet, or watching TV, or doing whatever else; in the wilderness, when the darkness descends, there's little else to do other than sleep.

I suppose if I'd had the foresight to bring a book along on the trip, I might've been able to keep myself awake until a little while longer; my torch shining on the pages.

But, sooner or later, the crushing silence—the total absence of all those droning, everyday sounds of human industry—takes its toll. Almost as if Mother Nature herself lulls you to sleep.

Peaceful . . . thick . . . rich . . . and—if Mother Nature had her way—*never-ending* . . .

That night, unlike the other nights following Petra's death, it was easy to find sleep.

Perhaps it was because I had managed to solve one of the

riddles; the one which'd seen my friends transformed into something other than themselves.

Into twisted, tormented—*demented*—versions of themselves.

Now I could see their motivations it wasn't quite such a mystery.

The police needed to come to bear on Petra's death. To draw unbiased conclusions.

The warmth of Eric and Alex's sleeping bodies was soothing against the chilly night-time air, and I'm certain that I might've slept for the entirety of the night if I hadn't been woken around dawn by something stirring outside the tent. It was a reflex, nothing more.

Outside, I heard the *snap* of a branch.

Or the *crackle* of a dead leaf underfoot.

When I turned to look over Alex and Eric, I saw only Eric there, lying on his back, mouth latched open, breathing heavily; his cheeks puffed out. Alex's sleeping bag was empty.

On my knees, I made my way to the tent flap. When I reached for the zip, I caught an odd, tingling sensation down my spine to think of the prospect of waking Eric. I wondered if this was how fledgling mothers and fathers might feel about waking a sleeping baby.

Picking their way out of the room ever so carefully.

Once out at the campsite, and with the first glow of the sunrise creeping up over the horizon, I made out the shapes of the tents. And then the figure of Alex.

Before I had the chance to fully absorb the scene, to note that Alex was crouched down beside the tent inside of which lay Petra's body, I heard a distinct *thud* from within.

My heart raced.

Sweat suddenly—*inexplicably*—dampened my face.

I scanned the tent for the sign of a silhouette.

Knowing that the sound had come from within.

From where Petra lay.

I snapped my attention back onto Alex. Saw that he was moving quickly. Keeping himself down low so that he wouldn't be spotted by whoever was inside the tent.

And then a figure emerged from within.

I spotted him immediately.

Without a doubt.

The rain cape was a giveaway.

The drifter.

Before so much as a thought had had the opportunity to skitter through my mind, I snapped upwards, staggered forwards, only recalling my twisted ankle when I landed all my weight on it.

I winced.

Sunk my teeth into my bottom lip.

Tasted blood.

Then urged myself onwards.

As I passed by the tent flap—sending a flashing, momentary image of an unattended wound through my mind—I caught a whiff of the stench.

Of decomposition.

Of rotting flesh.

It took everything within me to keep the fish from the day before down in my stomach.

I turned my attention back front and centre.

As I limped on, I noted Alex giving chase to the drifter.

But the drifter was far faster than either I or Alex had given him credit.

Soon enough, the drifter had bounded his way free of the campsite.

Disappeared up into the copse of Scots pines.

I observed Alex disappear, too, and thought to call out to him.

To urge him to return.

But it was too late.

Alex was, apparently, determined to pursue the drifter.

My ankle throbbing, and knowing that I would offer little in a chase, I turned around and made my way back to the campsite. When I got there, I saw Eric emerging from the tent.

Although it was clear that he had just got up—still rubbing the sleep from his eyes—he was also alert; glancing about himself, obviously trying to piece together just what had gone on here. He stumbled a couple of times as he made an effort to stand back up on his two feet.

His eyes were wide when they met mine.

And then they slipped onto the tent.

Where Petra's body lay.

Eric had hardly formed the word . . . *Who?* . . . before I answered him.

"The drifter," I said. "He was here."

All we had for breakfast was the trout which the drifter had caught the day before. It seemed somewhat odd for us to be chewing our way through the cold, rubbery fish at first light, but there was nothing we could do. We could only wait. Wait for Alex to return.

. . . Would the drifter be back?

It wasn't until around nine o'clock when Alex came back to the campsite.

He had deep, dark bags clinging to the bottoms of his eyes and I saw that he had several tears in his shirt and jeans. I guessed he had given as good of a chase as he could manage . . . but had fallen short. As he closed in, he shook his head. "Just disappeared," he said. "Got away so quickly."

He glanced back to the tent where Petra's body lay. His complexion visibly paled.

At least me and Eric had had the presence of mind to zip it back shut again. In the end, it'd taken both of us to do it, each one covering their mouth and nostrils with the neck of their shirt.

Shoulders slouching, and with a dour expression, Alex settled down on one of the logs opposite us. He glanced down at one of the fish, grimaced, and then held his head in his hands.

Deciding that one of us needed to offer Alex some sort of consolation, I elected myself . . . for no other reason than having the 'feminine' touch. I laid my fish down on the log, then went over, settling beside him. Because gentle acts never come all that naturally to me, I hesitated several moments before reaching my arm around Alex's shoulders.

I was aware that I probably stunk *strongly* of fish.

At least Alex was polite enough not to react.

He turned into me, nudging into my chest as if I was his mother, or something.

We sat like that, nobody saying anything, for what must have been ten or twenty minutes.

Finally, breaking the silence, his words dampened as he spoke into my fleece, Alex said, ". . . The hatchet."

"Hmm?" I said, looking down at him.

Alex unfurled himself from my hold.

He blinked away the watery film which lingered over the surface of his eyes.

"He took the hatchet," he said.

"The drifter?" I replied.

And then—as if I'd prompted him to—he drew back the

sleeve of his jumper to show me a scrape. "I was lucky," Alex continued. "I turned just in time—before he got the chance to have a proper chop at me." He shook his head. "Could've killed me if I hadn't run off then."

Again, I cursed the fact that we hadn't brought so much as rudimentary medical supplies with us on the trip. But, then again, the scrape didn't look all that bad. Hopefully Alex had had a tetanus booster recently.

Alex pulled the sleeve of his jumper back down.

I wondered what all this might mean.

I turned to Eric and Alex. "What was he doing here?" I said. "I mean, rooting about in the tent? I thought he'd slipped off somewhere else . . . bedded himself down someplace."

"Guess not," Alex said, speaking through a sigh.

I caught Eric's eye.

"What does it mean?" Eric said.

"What?" I replied.

Eric turned his hands over and inspected his palms. "Now that the hatchet's gone . . . the *thing* that Petra used to kill herself with . . . no evidence."

I thought about it for a moment, maybe two . . . that was all I needed. "How about we just tell the truth?" I said. "When Mercy and Graeme get back with the police we just tell them *the truth*."

Unsurprisingly, given how my 'friends' had acted throughout this episode so far, this option wasn't greeted with much enthusiasm. Then something else struck me.

I turned to Eric and Alex. "Mercy and Graeme *have* gone to get the police, haven't they?"

This time it was Alex who replied. "Of course they have," he said.

But I couldn't say I was convinced.

I decided not to mention anything else of the matter.

I looked to Alex again. "Did the drifter take anything else?"

"Not that I saw," Alex replied.

Just the thought of going back into that tent to confirm or deny this statement sent a shiver down the back of my neck. I wondered if I was still in shock, if I was still getting over the—*not insignificant*—experience of having seen my first dead body.

. . . Never mind that it had been one of my friends . . . or, at the very least, a *close* acquaintance.

"So," Eric said, "you think we just wait for Mercy and Graeme to show back up?"

I stared out over the loch, losing myself in the hypnotising, silvery, multi-coloured pattern of the surface. "I don't think there's a lot else we *can* do."

Paranoia?

That *night* none of us slept.
      Every slight stirring.
Every out-of-place bird chirping.
Every breath of wind.
I remained alert.
Ready.

We had little in the way of weapons, other than the walking pole which Eric had chivalrously donated to me. I held it tight across my chest, preparing myself for the giveaway silhouette of the drifter standing over the tent. The hatchet grasped tightly in his fist. Bringing it down upon us . . . hacking each and every one of us to pieces out here.

Where no one would hear our screams.

I felt an unshiftable weariness harness my mind.

Prevent me getting my thoughts straight.

Every time that I tried to think through our situation—to second guess Graeme, Mercy, Eric, Alex's motives—I came up against a brick wall in my brain.

Something which I simply couldn't move.

I found myself calling into question absolutely everything, examining the entirety of my experiences from the past few days; holding it all up to the light.

Trying to see what fit.

And what didn't . . .

But I could get no closer to the truth, no matter how hard I tried.

Finally realising that I wouldn't find sleep, I shifted out of the tent, poked my feet into my walking boots. I slipped out of the tent, drawing the flap shut behind me. Leaving the sleepers.

I hoped that they'd be unharmed when I returned.

They were innocents . . . most likely.

I used the walking pole to keep the worst of my weight off my ankle. Even now—even days later—it continued to feel as if someone constantly held blazing-hot coals up against my skin. I wondered if it was worse than a sprain, if I had broken it . . . and then I wondered if I'd be able to get out of this place by walking.

Maybe, when the police came, they would arrive by helicopter.

Did the police around here have access to a helicopter?

What would be the procedure for dealing with a dead body?

. . . What would be the procedure for dealing with us?

I slowly loped my way along the shore of the loch, listening to the early-morning birds chirping away as the sun rose again.

Graeme and Mercy hadn't arrived yet.

They had been gone for well over a day now.

No sign of them.

As I made it through a copse of Scots pines, and over onto another shore, away from our campsite, I wondered what could've happened to them. My mind filled with all sorts of imaginings; that one or both of them had fallen into a ditch, broken their leg . . . or that they'd taken a wrong turn and dropped down a cliff face. Perhaps they had made it back to the village, made it to the police, who hadn't believed their story. Or, worse, maybe the police had locked them up, waiting for their parents to come and fetch them.

But the most obvious of them all was also the most likely . . . that Graeme and Mercy hadn't gone to the police at all. That, for whatever reason, they had only *said* they were going to the police as some sort of a ruse to placate me. Well, it had worked in a way, hadn't it?

I scolded myself for being so gullible, lowering myself down onto the pebble shore, so that I could look out over the water and pretend that the campsite—*our campsite*—didn't even exist.

That I was the only living soul for miles and miles around.

I knew then that I would never return on a venture such as this. But if there had been a Next Time, I should have liked to do it alone. To allow myself to be submerged by solitude.

With that thought on my mind, I heard approaching footsteps.

The *scrub* of pebbles on pebbles.

I turned.

Saw the drifter.

Approaching me.

His rain cape had become torn; perhaps from the pursuit he had shared with Alex the day before. But my eyes soon moved beyond the state of his rain cape, and down to the object which he clasped in his hand, down at his thigh.

The hatchet.

Even in the dim light, I could make out the rusty-brown colour smeared onto the cutting edge, and onto the cheek of the hatchet.

Petra's blood.

I held myself very still.

Felt my heart thump in my throat.

No matter how hard I tried, I couldn't read the drifter's expression.

He seemed neutral.

Unaffected.

And his intention with the hatchet was not clear.

I gripped the walking pole tighter.

Feeling the sturdy wood in my grip sent a pang of confidence through my bloodstream.

I brought it up to my chest, ready to strike if required.

The drifter stepped closer.

That hatchet still at his side.

Only inches away now.

I breathed in the heady, musky scent.

Rabbit.

Fish.

. . . *Earth*.

It was all there, clinging to him.

How long had he lived out here—in the middle of nowhere . . .

How long had he been *waiting*?

He came to a halt standing only a step or two away from me.

I kept my eyes fixed on the hatchet, and then, because it felt as if there was no other option, I brought my gaze up to his. And we regarded one another.

I never would've guessed the thoughts which might've trickled through his brain.

Gently, with a tenderness I found unnerving, more because it was unexpected than unpleasant, the drifter held the hatchet out to me.

His fist clenched around it.

And then, because it seemed the obvious thing to do, I took it from him.

For several more seconds, we stood there—in silence—regarding one another.

I tried to think of what to do next . . . and came up with nothing.

What *was* I supposed to do?

I held the walking pole in one hand and the hatchet in the other.

Now I had all the power.

All the brute-force strength.

And yet, I still felt that the drifter—if he wished it so—could easily overwhelm me.

He was a master of this environment.

He was at home here.

While *I* was at home in civilisation.

The drifter remained where he was another moment, and then he backed away, turning around. I watched his shoulders, concealed beneath the rain cape, as he left me behind. As he disappeared back into the copse of Scots pines . . . to wherever it was he was headed.

Leaving me alone.

With the walking pole.

And the hatchet.

———

When I trod my way back to the campsite, I realised that I could hear voices.

And not the voices of Eric or Alex.

At first, I thought I might be imagining them . . . that I

might've somehow conjured them from some deep recess of my mind.

I clung onto the hatchet and the walking pole.

As if they might be able to help me.

I was struck by the lack of colour.

How the pair of black uniforms blended in with the landscape.

With the shore of the loch.

My eyes soon fell on Alex and Eric.

Each of them sitting where they had been previously.

On their logs.

When Alex and Eric turned their attention to me, the pair of black uniforms followed. And I felt their ice-cool eyes settle across me. And I felt their gaze take in what I carried with me; the hatchet, and the walking pole.

If they had had weapons, they might've drawn them.

If we had been in the middle of some built-up area, they might've demanded I drop the walking pole and the hatchet. But, as it was, they merely followed me with their eyes as I trod ever closer.

It was only when I was mere paces away that I thought long and hard about gripping those two implements. Just losing myself. Going crazy with the walking pole.

With the hatchet.

But I held my calm.

Told myself that I *had* to be calm.

The time for madness was over.

Locked-Up

Away

E xposed cinder blocks around me.
	I could feel their gentle chill.

It brought my skin up into goose pimples.

I could still taste the sweet, nourishing notes of chicken soup in my mouth—the soup which the police served me upon arrival at the station. I continued to feel it twisting away in my gut. Keeping me warm. Restoring me to some sort of life.

I reached out and brushed my fingertips against the white paper suit which the police had issued me with. They had taken away my own clothes when I'd got here, sealed them in a transparent, plastic bag. They had done the same with Eric and Alex too.

When they brought me in, they took my fingerprints. I had been hardly aware, off in some other place, as the officer had eased my fingers onto some inky mat before helping me to roll them onto a piece of paper.

A tiny trickle of light passed in through the frosted glass of the cell.

I could see that it was dim outside.

That the light was weak.

Daybreak?

Nightfall?

I had no idea.

I had been sleeping—*waiting*.

Wondering what would come next.

In the corridor outside the holding cell, I could hear footsteps.

The *jangle* of keys.

Then the push and prod of the keys in the lock.

The *clickety-clack* of the mechanism.

When the door brushed open, it sent fluorescent, strikingly bright white light dancing over me. It stung my eyes. I squeezed my eyes shut. Waited

. . . And then I heard the soft, male voice.

"Is there anybody you'd like to call?"

I thought about the question for several moments.

And then I replied.

"No," I said. "Nobody."

"Your parents?"

"No."

Another still, brooding silence.

I felt almost as if it tickled my skin.

As if it brought the tiniest of chuckles to the back of my throat.

Because if I couldn't find some humour in this situation then what was the alternative?

"We'd like to ask some questions," the voice said.

I pressed my lips tightly together—the light still overwhelming; making it impossible for me to see anything other than the linoleum floor beneath my feet.

"The doctor said you're going to be fine. Just a little shaken. She'll be in to see you once we're through with the questions, okay?"

"Okay," I replied.

I understood the situation, of course.

I had been formally arrested.

I needed to do what they said.

Under the officer's—the *detective's?*—watchful gaze, I rose up.

And I felt the officer's not-uncaring hands wrap my wrists with a pair of handcuffs.

I heard the gentle *click* as the cold steel embraced my flesh.

A slight pinch.

Slowly, the detective led me along the corridor, away from the holding cell.

Since the light was near-blinding, I had little option other than to bow my head, to keep my eyes on the slick, strangely sparkling blue floor of the corridor.

As the detective brought me to the interview room, I felt an odd, unplaceable urge to run away. To *break out* of this station . . . of where I had been *brought*.

But I kept calm.

Refused to allow myself to be swept away by madness.

I focussed on the pair of chairs—one opposite the other—and then the table between.

Waiting for the detective's prompt, seeing the outstretched arm indicating the chair furthest from the door, I did what I had to.

I settled in the chair.

Plastic.

Hard.

Thoroughly *unnatural.*

After a week or so of sitting on logs . . . of being out in the wilderness . . . it just felt intrinsically wrong. As if, maybe, all humankind had gone wrong somewhere.

I clutched my hands in my lap and waited, watching, as the detective shut the door behind himself, turned, and then took a seat opposite me.

I thought about all the TV shows I'd seen down the years. I thought about all the *films*. I wondered if the detective was going to scatter a cascade of photographs on the table. Photographs of the crime scene. And that he would get in my face. *Demand* to know everything I recalled about Petra . . . about the *crime* itself.

"So, Charlotte," the detective said, his voice as cool as it had been all along; his eyes set intently on my own. "Let's talk about what you remember, shall we?"

———

The room was featureless—*windowless*.

There were porcelain tiles—what I *believed* to be porcelain tiles—beneath my feet.

As I listened to what the detective had to say, I took in his appearance . . . his neat, coal-black suit. The crisp, clean, *white* shirt which he wore underneath. The black tie knotted about his throat. If it hadn't been for the identification tag clipped onto the breast pocket of his suit, I might've mistaken him for a funeral director.

The detective spoke, and spoke, and spoke.

This, again, was at odds with my experience of the police as told to me through mass media. I thought that I was going to be required to open up. That the detective would merely sit back and have me spill all the beans . . . and yet, what sort of beans did he expect me to spill?

I tuned back into his words; nausea squeezing my stomach:

". . . They've all given us the same story, Charlotte, they all say that they saw you . . . that *you* did it . . . that you held them at the campsite until two managed to escape, to get in touch with the police . . . all we need is a confession, okay? Just tell us the truth, what really went on, and then we'll take it from there . . ."

Something about what the detective said caught my attention.

I tilted my head back.

Took him in.

He stopped speaking.

" 'The truth' ?" I said. "You want to hear the truth?"

"That's right, Charlotte."

It felt as if something tickled my chest from within.

As if my breathing was being restricted in some way.

Like somebody might be hugging me from behind.

Squeezing the air out of me.

"Petra killed herself," I said, my voice low, doleful.

The detective leaned back in his chair.

Crossed his arms.

Then, slowly—*surely*—he shook his head.

"No, Charlotte, she didn't. That would be inconsistent with the findings of our analysis."

I tilted my head upwards, away from my hands, writhing in my lap.

"It would've been near impossible for Petra to use the axe on herself."

"It's not an axe," I said. "It's a *hatchet*."

The detective nodded as if this detail didn't matter. If he believed that *this* detail didn't matter then what other details might've been merely 'insignificant' for him?

How could I trust *anything* he said?

Perhaps he was just as bad as the others . . . as Eric, Alex, Graeme and Mercy . . .

Still, I tried to focus in on that which mattered.

"They told me that she killed herself," I said.

Again, the detective shook his head.

I waited for him to add some sort of explanation.

But he had nothing else to say, apparently.

"They said," I went on, "that I *drove* her into killing herself."

The detective continued to look on at me, his gaze slow and steady, and unmoving.

It was clear that he wouldn't allow me out of his sight.

That he didn't *trust* me . . .

But why?

What reason had I given to *anybody* that I wasn't to be trusted?

"Listen to me, Charlotte," the detective said. "On that *hatchet*, the murder weapon, we found all sorts of fingerprints. All sorts of DNA. Inside of the tent we found more DNA. Other items which we consider to be evidence. But the only account—the only *real* piece of evidence which we have to go on—is your entrance on the crime scene . . . the pair of officers who arrived there, they saw you approach them with that branch hanging from your hand . . . with that axe down at your side." He dropped his voice. "Blood still smearing its blade."

I felt something spark up within me.

"It was a walking pole," I said. "Eric crafted it. And"—I felt my voice quivering a little, with something like anger—"it was a *hatchet*."

The detective held up his hands, exposing his palms.

Tilting back slightly in his chair.

The gesture reminded me of a child, back at school.

However, through these wonderings, something leaped out at me.

"The others," I said. "Did you let them go?"

The detective frowned and then shook his head vigorously. "Oh, no," he replied. "Of course not . . . they're suspects as much as you yourself are."

After I heard those words tumble out through his lips, I found it almost impossible to tune my attention back into the matter at hand. To so much as think about who might've killed Petra. Because, on my mind, I had the unshakeable knowledge that it was me against them.

And I was determined I would be the one to triumph . . . if that was even the correct word.

———

About an hour later, after the detective had asked me question after question, willing me on into giving up some scrap of vital information—something which would lead to a breakthrough in this case—I was finally allowed to return to the holding cell.

For the first time, I really took in my surroundings.

The concrete bunk with the flimsy, thin, plastic-laminated mattress on top. And then, as the door shut closed behind me, the window; struck with the flickering orange of the streetlights outside.

I gently allowed myself to slump down on the mattress, to feel the rigid form of the cement moulded beneath. As I brought my feet up, allowing my mind to slip away to some other place—to some *nicer, more distant* place—I felt a smile begin to take hold of my mouth. To manipulate my lips, and, almost by proxy, to raise my spirits.

Because, for the first time in this entire episode, it felt as if I had more information than the others. It felt almost as if *I* would be the one in the loop from here on out.

Or maybe I was just deceiving myself.

Throughout the time I spent on my own, in the holding cell, I found myself building up strange, malevolent images of my former 'friends'. I saw them as twisted, messed-up versions of themselves. I spent a long while trying to work out how they had done it; how they had managed to manipulate the situation so that even the police believed I'd been the one to kill Petra.

I scolded myself for having—so willingly—bent to their will.

Allowed them to keep me right where they wanted me.

But there was something.

Still something.

The detective had told me that my 'friends' were still suspects.

It was some sort of consolation to know that they wouldn't get off so lightly.

Or would they?

I slept not at all; only drifting away into the shallower portions of my mind in what must've been the early hours of the morning. I saw so many things . . . but mainly blood.

On my hands.

A reddish brown.

Sticky.

Impossible to clean . . .

I tried as hard as I could to tempt those images out of my mind—the ones which surrounded that fateful, drunken night. I tried to shed new light on the matter . . . beyond that conversation I'd had with Petra; when I'd unwittingly perhaps underscored and validated her desire to do away with herself.

The others held me responsible, whatever happened; even if Petra had, somehow, against the police's better judgement, managed to kill herself with the hatchet.

Did it matter to them if I'd been the one to wield the weapon, or if Petra herself had been the one to hack away at her own throat?

. . . It didn't seem so.

Unless, of course, they were attempting to cover their own backs.

That could *well* be a theory.

When I heard the footsteps again outside the holding cell, I had some odd premonition that it would be Graeme standing there, holding the keys, ready to walk in through the door. I had strange, greatly out-of-place fantasies between the two of us.

Sexual fantasies.

And yet, even as they felt so real to me, I knew that they could be nothing other than a symptom of my disoccupied mind.

I waited . . . and waited.

And finally the door opened.

Gone For Good

L egs *dangling off* the edge of my thin mattress, I rocked my
feet back and forth beneath me, listening to the gentle
creak-creak of the bed springs.

I glared up at the barred window of my prison cell.

I had been lucky—the wardens were always keen to remind
me of that fact.

Most other prisoners were lucky to have a window out in the
corridor.

Let alone one in their own cell.

The window, of course, was far too high up for me to get a
look out of.

Even if I'd clambered up onto the top bunk—onto my cellmate Greta's bed—I wouldn't have been able to see much more
than a scrap of the overcast Scottish sky.

The trial had passed like a whirlwind, too quickly for me to
make sense of all the intricacies, of all the consequences. I could
still recall listening to my 'friends' standing up in court; speaking

out against me. Jabbering lies about me. Telling the whole room —*the judge*—what a monster I was.

And how, that fateful night, with my belly swilling with liquor, I had done that which I had—apparently—threatened so often.

Maybe, in retrospect, I'd treated the entire episode far too lightly.

Perhaps I shouldn't have struck the cool, chill façade that'd seen me demonised in all the papers—the local and national news.

My lawyer, paid for by my parents, had often told me to 'lighten up' or to 'cry a little' once I got to court. But it was all I could do to keep myself conscious, to not simply drop to the ground in some sort of Regency woman's faint . . . and to lie there till Time Immemorial.

I never expected any other verdict.

What could I hope for when there were four others to speak out against me?

That one of them might snap to their senses and do the 'right' thing?

That they might tell the truth?

. . . No, I knew that 'telling the truth' as a virtue had been proven to me—*over and over*—as a fallacy. When the choice between 'telling the truth' and 'saving one's skin' cropped up, I knew which side would win out time and time again.

I would never repeat *that* mistake.

"You think you could shut the hell up?"

I turned my attention upwards, to Greta, lying on her back on the bunk above mine. Her blond hair was buzzed short to a centimetre, maybe two. She was built like a fridge with the sleeves of her overalls slashed at the shoulders, showing off the pair of inky blue serpents entwined down one arm; the long, winding path up to a mansion on a hill on the other.

When I'd asked her about these tattoos, she'd just grunted.

Said something about needing to 'find herself'.

I hadn't prompted her for further explanation.

She leafed through a paperback copy of *The Bible*. Some nuns had been in to see us earlier today, dispensing a copy to each and every one of us. For whatever reason—'good behaviour' ?—me and Greta had been allowed to keep our copies.

Greta continued to read, not so much as casting a warning glare in my direction.

I realised that Greta was complaining about the *creak-creak* of the mattress springs as I rocked my legs back and forth. In an attempt to placate her, I ceased doing it.

I took care not to make so much as a sound as I brought my legs up onto my bed, and then spread them out ahead of me. There was about an hour until we would be forced into Recreation Time; when we would have the chance to go outside for an hour or so, to 'stretch our legs'. Despite what the others might've thought—the other women—I couldn't muster much in the way of enthusiasm for the time period. In fact, if it'd been permitted, I would've much preferred the peace and quiet of my cell, devoid of Greta for an hour or more, over the supposed benefit of 'fresh air'.

But expressing opinions such as these would only lead to suspicion.

Both from the wardens and from other prisoners.

And, as I had learned early on in my days at HM Prison Highlands, it was better not to attract attention; positive or negative.

Better not to put anybody's nose out of joint.

Better just to do as I was told.

I lay back on the bed and stared up at the pattern of springs beneath Greta's mattress above. Greta had a reading pattern. As she turned each page of her bible, she would snort up a whole wad of phlegm. Swallow it back. Sniff a couple of times. And then she'd just go on reading.

The first I knew of the visitors was the clanking turn of the locking mechanism.

I didn't even hear the footsteps outside the cell.

I moved quickly, straightening into a standing position.

Greta did the same.

Dropping *The Bible* on her mattress.

Throwing herself off the top bunk.

Landing beside me.

The two of us stared at the door.

At the warden who stood there.

"Charlotte Connolly," the warden said.

I felt a lump form in my throat.

But I managed to nod.

"Come with me, please."

———

The warden led me past the other cells.

I felt the eyes all lingering on me—surely, if they could get their hands on me, they would've torn me to pieces. I knew, when I returned to my cell, I would suffer some kind of panic attack. I wouldn't know where the attack would come from . . . but I would feel certain that there *would* be one to come. In their eyes, I would need to be taught a 'lesson' for attracting such attention.

For having brought this fuss upon myself.

The warden took me through several secure doors, and then, on the other side, cuffed my wrists. She then led me along another corridor bringing me finally to a halt outside what appeared to be quite a tight room. She knocked twice, waited for the response within, and then turned the doorknob. She stood back, shepherding me inside.

My heart rapped against my ribs.

I felt a chill pass through my bloodstream.

But I forced myself onwards.

Inside the room, I found myself confronted with a woman dressed in a smart trouser suit. She clutched her hands on the cheap-looking desk and wore an understanding smile. Her head cocked slightly to one side. There was a plastic chair standing before the desk, and, looking to the warden, I trod over to it. And took a seat there.

I allowed my cuffed hands to dangle between my knees.

All this earned me was a reprimand from the warden.

Responding, I brought my hands back up onto my lap.

Where they could be clearly seen.

I turned my attention onto the woman in the trouser suit, seeing that her smile hadn't—*apparently*—shifted from her face. She seemed assured here, in the prison. That was uncommon. It was unlike other visitors I had seen:

The curious legal students taking guided tours.

The doctors or nurses called into action afterhours.

The young girls—young *offenders*—brought along to be shown where they would be headed if they didn't behave themselves.

I caught a whiff of something like honey on the air, and I realised it must be the woman's perfume. Her makeup. In prison such items were not permitted. Even wardens were reverent to this rule . . . or maybe they just didn't want to draw attention to themselves, like the prisoners.

The woman held her hand out across the desk. "Pleased to meet you, Charlotte. My name's Daniella."

I looked at her hand. It was so soft, apparently well-mois-turised.

Well taken care of.

I shrugged my shoulders, bringing my cuffed hands up so that Daniella could see.

Daniella aimed a glance at the warden, nodded to her, and the warden, with a slight sigh, descended on me and undid the handcuffs. When the warden retreated from my side, I noticed that she didn't return to where she'd been standing before, but stood a half dozen steps closer . . . so that she could come to Daniella's aid in an emergency. If the prisoner refused to behave herself.

Now, I finally took Daniella's hand, shook.

It felt extremely odd to be touching skin so soft; so untarnished by time *inside*.

Daniella seemed to note this too, when she slipped her fingers away from mine.

For the first time in the entire encounter, she seemed to become somewhat timid. She coughed then bent down below the desk. As she did so, the warden leaned into me, ready if I tried anything.

Perhaps the warden should've checked over my file a little closer—if there was anything she would find about me, it was that, throughout my two-year stay, I had proven myself to be an unremarkable inmate. Despite my supposed crime.

Daniella returned to her sitting position with a whole wad of papers. She slapped them down on the desk in a way which made me flinch. "We've been looking into your case, Charlotte."

"Have you?" I replied, surprised that I felt nothing at all.

I could still recall the first days at the prison, hoping—*praying*—that a day such as this would come. That someone would turn up; that someone would come to tell me that they *understood* . . . that they'd noted the injustice.

That would've been all I required.

But, I suppose, perhaps like others who've been wrongly incarcerated—who truly knows?—I decided I *deserved* to be in prison for one reason or another. In the time I'd spent locked up, I'd convinced myself that there *had* to be some reason for this situation.

That was a difficult mentality to shift once established.

"We've found some interesting inconsistencies."

Daniella flipped through the pages, came to a halt. She slipped the warden a glance, and the warden gave her a nod in reply—clearly granting her permission; almost as if this trouser-suited woman had been an inmate herself. The woman passed one of the pages over to me.

I took it from her.

My vision was unfocussed.

The lines of text all blurred.

Running into one another.

But I could just about make out the lengthy, highlighted sections.

It was only then that I realised I was crying.

"Oh, dear," Daniella said, digging about in her jacket pocket before producing some tissues.

This, again, had to go through the warden, who swiftly dug through the tightly wadded ball, and, apparently establishing nothing untoward was being passed to me, allowed me to take the tissues.

I pressed them to my tear ducts, trying to stop the waterworks flowing.

But it seemed to be in vain.

When I'd got my head around going to prison, I'd believed that I would most likely cry every day. But, instead, the opposite had proven true. I'd somehow found some part of myself—something locked away *deep*—where I could go to . . . and, strangely, it was still that wide-open, middle-of-nowhere shore of the loch. Just sitting there, perhaps dangling my bare toes into the freezing water, staring out at the hillside surrounding, forgetting myself.

Forgetting *everything*.

It was a sort of outpouring of all that I'd kept bottled up for the past couple of years. All those times when I'd wished to crumple myself into a ball and to give up on everything. On *everybody*.

Because they had already given up on me.

"Charlotte?" Daniella said, once I'd brought the clenched tissues down from my eyes. "I really think you have a good case for appeal here."

———

The strangest part about being in prison is the way gossip manages to get around.

Even though it'd only been me, Daniella, and the warden in the room, it seemed that, by the time the next morning rolled around, everybody knew about the appeal.

And, more than that, they knew the *confidence* held within the appeal.

That it wasn't like one of the standard situations . . . which was to say, it wasn't like I was attempting something in vain. For a start *they* had come to me.

Not the other way around.

Throughout our subsequent meetings, Daniella explained about how she'd got hold of the drifter; the one who Graeme and the others had been so keen to pin the 'murder' on. It had taken time—longer than two years of searching with very limited resources—but he had been tracked down in the end. And, through what was described to me as a 'strenuous' series of interviews, the drifter was gently led through his personal recollections of the matter.

During the process, Daniella and I were relocated to another, much larger room. It featured a window which looked down on a sunlit courtyard. The leaves of elm trees flickered in the gentle breeze, making the sunrays shimmer back at me . . . almost blinding with their brightness when I'd grown so accustomed to artificial light; and, mostly, to no light at all.

The warden, the same one as always, stood off over at the door of the room. She tapped away on her smartphone, clearly bored of the whole ordeal, and finally accepting that I wasn't going to make some ill-advised bid for freedom. Perhaps the warden, too, realised there was light to be had.

A hope which hadn't previously existed.

Daniella slapped paper upon paper, creating piles on the table before us. She tucked her hair behind her ear as she worked, her eyes constantly on the move, picking out this or that detail on the pages spread out there. I had to admit that I felt almost like a spare part in my standard position—no cuffs on my wrists; my arms folded across my chest.

Daniella had her organisational systems. Each pile meant a different stage of the appeals process. Each pile was concerned with shooting down specific parts of testimony—specific parts of *evidence*. All the statements my 'friends' had given in court—untruths about my relationship with Petra; with my secret *loathing* of her. My penchant to go after boys, creating complex fantasies before becoming aggressively defensive—*violent*—when said fantasies were challenged.

It was put to the court by my friends' lawyers that Petra had challenged these 'fantasies' of mine . . . that I'd held some sort of a longing for Graeme, and when Petra had had the tenacity to tell me the truth, that he couldn't give two shits about me, I'd panicked . . . mercilessly turning my wrath upon her . . . *punishing* Petra. This was the line of argument which'd seen me go to prison.

And the others go free.

Now, though, it appeared that a different picture was emerging.

Wanting to feel more involved in the process, I took to digging through one of Daniella's many piles. I made many promises that I wouldn't mess up any of the organisation; that I would put everything right back where I'd found it.

The entire purpose of the exercise was to highlight each and every one of the inconsistencies as my friends had spoken them in court. Their renderings of the night's events could then be compared to those of the drifter, as per his videoed statement.

It was that element which was most in doubt for me.

Even two years later, I could still recall how the drifter had been near incomprehensible in his speech. I couldn't quite imagine how Daniella and her team had managed to untangle anything that could be put to use on the case . . . then again, I knew that I had to be patient, and I had to trust in those who were greater qualified than me.

All of this might've been helped if I'd been able to recall more details of the fateful night. To be able to give a point-by-point description of just what'd gone on. My role in the unfurling events.

One thing was for certain, though, no matter how I scoured my memories—no matter how I held up my judgements—I knew that I was innocent; that I hadn't had anything to do with Petra's death.

Even, as drunk as I was, I knew I would recall such details.

All the forced remembering did for me was confirm, all the

more, that my 'friends' had something they all wanted to protect themselves from. And that I was the sacrificial lamb.

That left only the question—the question which, with Daniella's help, I was trying so hard to answer. Why would the others want Petra dead?

Of course I had told Daniella all about what Graeme had told me; about how they had dawdled in going to the police, wanting to get the 'story' straight . . . but in court this had been disregarded since the evidence I gave was proven to be unreliable.

I was a loose cannon.

Unworthy of credibility.

Throughout the pages and pages which Daniella had brought to me, I'd found myself consistently drawn back to those which concerned Mercy. Maybe it was Petra's dried blood on her wrist which stuck out in my mind. When I focussed in on Mercy's interviews—those typed-out pages which the police had extracted from her—I found many interesting notes.

There was one which concentrated on Mercy's relationship with Petra, and what they had known of one another.

In one of the first interviews conducted, Mercy had claimed that she'd not known Petra at all; and that her only real relationship to her was through Alex . . . and then, as I fished through another pile of papers, and brought out what was being termed a 'fifth' interview, I picked out a section in which Mercy went into quite some detail about a birthday party.

About *her* birthday party.

It seemed, at this point of the interview process, that Mercy had begun to feel somewhat more comfortable in the company of the police. Perhaps she had started to believe that she was no longer being considered a suspect, and that anything she said from then on would merely be used against me. Maybe that was the reason for her sloppiness.

In the statement, Mercy made specific reference to the fact that she had invited Petra to her birthday party. There was no mention of Alex at all.

Furthermore, there was an aside from Mercy about how they'd happened to share the same personal tutor at university. That they'd struck up a friendship while waiting to go in to see their tutor one day. Mercy went on to explain how she'd only learned *later* that Petra was Alex's girlfriend.

I glanced up, caught Daniella's eye for a moment as she was fishing through a certain pile. She smiled back at me, and I said nothing; unsure whether I'd found anything that would be of any significance.

Most likely, what with Daniella and her team being deeply competent at what they did, they had already seen what I saw . . . they had already considered its implications.

But, still, I read on.

As the interview proceeded, Mercy revealed more and more about Petra, neatly contradicting those early interviews in which she had claimed, before the trip, to only have known *of* Petra from a distance. And always only through Alex.

One highlighted section, in particular, was interesting.

In it, Mercy spoke about a—*false*—incident which she claimed to have witnessed. She spoke about how she'd been walking along with me when we'd bumped into Petra.

All of us had spoken together and Mercy kept bringing up, in the interview, how I had appeared to give Petra a sort of jilted glance as I'd taken her in . . . as if there was something about her clothing—her *appearance*—which I didn't like.

I knew this was all set up to presuppose my apparent *dislike* for Petra, so as to further my 'friends' claims that I would've had it in me to murder her so brutally.

The more that I read through Mercy's claims, the surer I became that I had uncovered the true murderer. The true psychopath. The one who, in my mind, was increasingly becoming the dangerous one to let free.

But, above all else, I could feel it becoming more and more of a fact that whatever had become of Petra, it certainly *hadn't* been a suicide.

Premeditated murder sounded *far* more likely.

Hope

I *tried not* to read too much into the line of enquiry I'd uncovered.

I merely presented my findings to Daniella, who, at first, treated these claims dubiously, before finally, looking me in the eye, began to take it seriously.

That day, when she left me behind at the prison, I recalled her swift exit.

How she'd seemed to almost *sweep* out of the room.

Unable to contain her enthusiasm at the breakthrough.

As for me, though, I returned to my prison cell—with my cellmate, Greta—and bided my time, knowing that it would do nothing for me to get my hopes up.

With nothing else to do in that featureless room—nothing except read *The Bible*, if I'd been that way inclined, if I wished to make my mother proud—I turned over the details of the case again and again in my mind; trying to get all the pieces to fit.

What became clearer and clearer to me was how Mercy had

set out—before we'd placed so much as a single foot on the path to Loch Monar—to *kill* Petra.

Premeditated murder.

. . . The *why* remained, though . . . but I was certain that, in among all those lies, was the answer.

It would just take some digging.

And, perhaps, a little perseverance.

Although I tried my very best to put the matter far from my mind, I couldn't help but imagine the scene—Mercy's *fury* as she'd grabbed hold of that hatchet and brought it down, time and time again, on Petra's throat. What had passed through her brain?

Had *anything* at all passed through her brain?

. . . But, above all else, I wanted to know why the others had covered this up.

Why the others had decided the guilty Mercy deserved to go free while I deserved to be punished.

One day, pawing through the piles of papers, Daniella let out a *shriek*.

To begin with, I thought that there was something wrong . . . that something she'd been working on had crumbled down into nothing.

At this stage of the process, with several of the provisional steps already booked in, one single piece of evidence—*one assumption too many*—might grind the entire enquiry to a halt.

However, I soon realised that Daniella was going through Graeme's interviews.

And that she was looking over one particular date.

She looked to me, above the rims of the thick-rimmed glasses she would keep tucked in the breast pocket of her trouser suit when not in use. Normally, when speaking, that was where they would stay. "Did you know anything about this?" she said.

"Hmm," I replied, casting a glance over to the distracted warden by the door, and not having a clue what sort of a track Daniella had gone off along.

When I came around behind her, looked down over the page, I saw where Daniella had highlighted several lines from an interview with Graeme.

And, specifically, I read mentions Graeme made to a 'past relationship' with Petra.

This was as much news to me as Mercy's past friendship with Petra.

Daniella met my eye, her whole body seeming to tremble slightly. "Within this testimony, Graeme speaks about how the two of them had a 'thing'."

"A 'thing'?" I replied, my tone a little hesitant.

Maybe it was the playground language being bandied about.

Daniella nodded, turned her attention back downwards, to the transcript. "When asked if he knew Petra previously, he admitted that he had done. When asked to describe the nature of the relationship, he admits that they had had a 'thing' during the first week of university." She paused, eyed me for a long moment. "During Freshers' Week."

I sketched my mind back to Freshers' Week—my first week at university.

It wasn't something that was easily done.

In many ways, it was a false start; the sparks of friendship between strangers who, in the coming weeks, would realise that, really, they hadn't all that much in common aside from being thrown together by the quirky lottery of accommodation allocation. I'd ended up with a my first-year next-door neighbour, a girl called Nathalie. I remembered how the two of us went about campus, checking the place out. How we visited the sign-ups for various clubs and societies; neither of us bothering to join anything. Nathalie had been studying chemistry. While I'd been studying geography. Once our courses had commenced, we had just sort of drifted apart.

That'd been the end of it . . .

As for the first week of university itself, well, I couldn't say that I remembered anything at all about the people around me. Not beyond my immediate course mates. I hadn't yet forged something like friendship with Eric, Graeme, Mercy or Alex.

I turned back to Daniella. "I don't remember anything," I replied, finally.

Daniella's attention moved back to the transcript before her, nodding, apparently already having figured as much. A dead-end . . . for now.

The two of us went back to our leafing through the transcripts until one of the wardens came to fetch me. To bring me back to my cell.

———

That night, after lights out, I lay back on my bunk.

I stared up at the weave of the springs in the mattress above.

Then I heard Greta stirring.

In the gloom, I made out Greta's eyes looming through the darkness.

Picking me out.

"Charlie?" she said.

Although it was rare for the two of us to speak—let alone for *Greta* to be the one to initiate conversation—I decided to cover up my surprise . . . and, to some extent, my *happiness* that she wanted to speak. I'd seen the girls Greta hung around. All muscles. Mean faces. Tattoos all over the place. I didn't particularly want to get too close to *that* crowd.

"Uh-huh," I replied, nonchalantly.

"You kill that girl?"

"What?"

"That girl, you know, all this appeal stuff you're going through—did you do it or not?"

I paused for several seconds.

Felt my heart swell in my throat.

"No," I said. "I didn't."

There was a long silence in the cell.

I could hear Greta's heavy-smoker breathing.

Then, "If you say so."

I heard creak of the mattress above as Greta turned on her side, apparently going off to sleep.

I had beaten the point where I'd wanted to convince other prisoners of my innocence. Sure, for the first few days, I'd wanted to make it clear that I *didn't* belong here. Soon enough, though, that'd proven just as effective a tactic as screaming 'I AM SPAR-TACUS!' at the top of my lungs.

It appeared one prison cliché held true.

Everybody was innocent.

As I lay there, dwelling on the night-time, I thought about the question Greta had asked me.

And then I studied the subtext.

What had she *really* been wanting to know?

Finally, I managed to pluck up the courage.

To go through with what I imagined was my end of this conversation.

"Greta?" I said.

There was a grunt in reply.

"You never told me what you did."

The silence was so long that I turned my attention to the

gentle sound of footfalls in the corridor outside. The wardens doing their evening rounds. Checking everything was in order.

From somewhere, I could hear dripping.

I turned my mind to wondering at what it might be:

Busted pipe?

Leaking toilet?

. . . Escaping blood?

When Greta replied to me, from the bunk above, it took me off guard.

So much so that I flinched.

"Petrol station," she said. "Middle of the night. Went in with these other two guys. The lead guy had a gun. The other two of us just had golf clubs. Could've been worse if we were armed too. Lead guy shot the worker on the till. Shot him dead. We made off with the cash—a car parked out on the forecourt. Police showed up about a week later. Somebody turned us in. My bet's on the other guy—the other guy who worked the job. One without the gun." She snorted, hard. Spat. "Wouldn't tell us, though. Wouldn't tell us *anything*."

I waited, staring into the darkness, feeling my heart beat against my ribcage.

I didn't quite know what I'd expected.

Maybe I'd thought Greta would be just like the others.

With another story to tell.

One which proved—*once and for all*—her innocence.

But, no, Greta had simply told the truth.

Nothing but cold, hard facts.

———

About a week later, and another week of poring over documents in Daniella's company, I was surprised to find the warden escorting me to a different location. We weren't headed for the meeting room where me and Daniella had been going through the paperwork previously.

When I asked where we were going, the warden simply told me that I had a visitor.

A *visitor?*

I studied the implications of this.

Wondered what it might mean.

My parents came by—*religiously*—once a week.

But only ever on Sundays.

I wondered if that was, maybe, some innovation of my mother's.

So that she might feel that she'd done a 'good' deed on God's day.

Sure enough, though, the warden led me on through the eggshell-painted corridors, past the many industrial-strength bars, and into the reception area for visitors.

It was a tight, windowless room with a camera up in the corner.

A cheap wooden table and a pair of blue plastic chairs.

I glanced to the warden, who indicated I should sit.

I turned my attention to the secure door.

The door which led to the outside world.

An electrically loaded lock buzzed somewhere out of sight.

The door opened on its automatic, hydraulic arm.

And a man stepped through.

It took me a moment to realise that it *was* a man.

Snowy-haired.

A poorly shaven, red-raw complexion.

He wore a suit which sagged off him.

It seemed like he'd lost weight but not yet got around to changing his wardrobe.

The man glanced to the warden, and then, as if he was putting it off as long as he could manage, he turned his attention downwards onto me. He had mournful, grey-blue eyes.

And he gave me something approaching a smile.

He took a seat.

Then glanced up, across the table, at me.

"Charlotte?" he said, as if he wanted to make sure he'd got the right person.

"Yes?" I replied.

"My name's Patrick—Patrick *Aldernaldy*."

It was like someone had punched me directly in the solar plexus.

My heart skipped a beat.

"Eric's dad?" I said.

He inclined his head.

Not even a full nod.

As if he was greatly aware of the security camera.

As if he was aware that he didn't want to give anybody any sort of incriminating evidence.

"What do you want?" I got out, finally.

I guess that prison had played havoc with my manners.

He blinked several times in rapid succession.

Then said, "I've come to speak about Eric."

"What *about* Eric?"

Again, he did that rapid-blinking thing.

He swallowed hard.

Could I see *tears* in his eyes?

"Last weekend," he said, "Eric was found . . . was found . . ."

Despite his wavering voice, how he could apparently not find the strength to continue, I managed to piece it all together. "Dead?" I said. "Eric's dead?"

Eric's father looked up now, meeting my eye.

He gave a doleful nod.

I breathed in the air of the visitors' room.

Unlike the rest of the prison, which stank of disinfectant—and, faintly, of *urine*—they kept this room well fragranced.

Was it lilies?

Or lemongrass?

I'd really lost all concept of smell during my time *inside*.

Eric's father hunched his shoulders up.

He bowed his head.

Sobbed quietly, his fist held up to his mouth.

I glanced over to the warden, watching us from the doorway.

Although I wanted to reach across, to console the man somehow, I knew that I couldn't.

Finally, he got himself together.

Made to get up off his chair.

It was only when he was about to press the button which would open the secure door that I thought to ask him one final question.

"How?" I said.

Eric's father didn't turn around, and the only word which I could understand through his nearly closed mouth was, "Suicide."

Then he was gone.

And I was on my way back to my cell.

Suicide?

Why would Eric commit *suicide*?

In Tatters

In the office, paperwork all spread out around us, I tried to get my head straight.

Daniella, of course, had been the first person I told about Eric's death. Somehow it seemed to have skipped her by. From the sounds of things, nothing of the details of Eric's death had made the news. His family, it seemed, had wanted to keep things as covered up as they were able to manage.

Before Daniella could make any comment on the matter, I couldn't help but break in with just what was on *my* mind. "I don't think it was suicide," I said.

Daniella stared down at a pile of papers before her. "No?" she said, her mind clearly elsewhere. "Why's that?"

"Doesn't fit," I replied, finally. "I mean, why would he do it?"

Daniella continued to stare down at the papers. She shrugged. "I don't know. It could've been one of a thousand things. Perhaps he didn't like his job . . . his life . . . relationship troubles." She glanced up at me, meeting my eye. "Maybe it was the guilt—the *knowledge*—of what they did . . . of whatever happened to Petra, his role in it."

I turned my thoughts to the jovial young man, with those khaki shorts of his, and the two of us heading up the slope, away from the campsite, in search of that wasps nest.

It was like looking through a veil into a former life.

To how things had been *before* we'd discovered Petra's body . .

.

I shook my head, locked onto Daniella's gaze. "And what if Mercy did it? What if she decided that he was dangerous—that he was thinking about sharing information? That he was . . ."

But my words faded away when I noticed Daniella's eyes slip away from mine.

"Danny?" I said. "What is it? What's on your mind?"

Daniella just continued to stare into nothingness for a while.

"Hello?" I said, and then, realising that she'd gone pale, I looked to the warden. "Could she have a glass of water?"

The warden reached for her walkie-talkie, jabbered away into its static.

I got up from my chair, went around the table, covered in all those papers which promised me a life beyond the walls of a prison. A *second* chance . . .

I reached out, squeezed her shoulders. "What is it, Danny?"

Her muscles were all drawn taut.

She was trembling slightly.

Finally, in a weak voice—almost a whisper—she raised herself up out of her seat. "I can't do this," she said. "I don't think I can *do* this."

Although I wanted, more than anything, to stop her striding determinedly to the door, I knew that there was nothing I could do. Anything that the warden witnessed which might pertain to aggression would be a black mark against my name.

Privileges—*privileges such as this one*—would be swiftly withdrawn.

All I could do was watch Daniella leave, and wait for the warden to escort me back to my cell.

———

A few days later I received an item of correspondence.

At least I could console myself with the fact that I still had *that* privilege; that whatever had gone on with Daniella a few days previously hadn't had an effect on my status in the eyes of the wardens.

It was a letter.

It bore the stamp of the legal-justice charity Daniella worked for.

And it detailed, simply—*clearly*—how, although it was most unfortunate, my appeal had been put on hold; owing to an 'issue' with a 'key piece of evidence'.

Of course it didn't take me long to put two and two together.

To figure out what'd gone wrong here.

That *Eric* had been the 'key piece of evidence'.

And that, now he was gone, it shattered the appeal.

As I sat on my bunk, listening to Greta snoring away—taking an afternoon nap—I read, and re-read, the letter over and over again; as if there was some nugget which I was missing. As if the solution to this whole mystery surrounding Petra's death might be there.

Ready for me to discover.

After a while, I crumpled the letter into a ball and tossed it into the toilet bowl.

I hesitated a moment before flushing it down.

But I knew it was for the best.

If I kept the letter with me, I would only obsess over it.

It would only drive me *crazy*.

From then on, I was in my cell for several weeks, waiting to hear anything about the appeal . . . anything about *anything* at all.

Throughout my incarceration, I'd got used to not being able to contact the outside world. But, at that time, it was indescribably frustrating not to have so much as a telephone; an email address.

For the first time during my stay at HM Prison Highlands, I admitted that I'd allowed myself to become dejected—*downbeat*. Because, if everyone on the outside had given up on me now —*forgotten about me*—then where was the will to continue?

Finally, the warden gave me word that Daniella had returned. However, instead of travelling to the office space we'd used for our investigations, this time I was led down to the visitors' area; as I had been when Eric's father had come to visit; to inform me of his son's death.

His son's 'suicide'.

In the visitors' area, I noted, for the first time, how skittish Daniella seemed. Although she would usually stow her glasses unless she was actually reading something, she wore them throughout our exchange. While we'd gone through the documents in one of the prison offices, I'd always held something of an admiration for Daniella; for how she carried herself with a certain grace. But, looking at her that day, in a smart trouser suit and with great, big dark circles beneath her eyes, I couldn't help but be put in mind of a sagging balloon.

Almost all the air gone from inside.

She did her best to smile at me, but I could tell, from the tone of her voice, that she was only putting on a brave face. "It's like this, Charlotte," she said, right after I'd sat down—not bothering with any sort of greeting. "Eric was going to come out against the others . . . he *agreed* to help with the case. To tell the truth." She gave a shake of her head, and I could see, from the watery quality of her eyes, that she was on the brink of tears. "These past few days, we've done all we can to go after the others—to get them to come forward . . . it's been *two years* now, you would have thought that they must be suffering from extreme guilt."

There was a pause and I saw my chance to put in a word.

"Yeah," I said, "or they've managed to convince themselves that I *did* really do it."

Daniella padded about inside her jacket, searching for something, apparently.

Before she got a chance to produce anything from within, I put in, "What about the drifter? You know, when you said that he had been videoed . . . that you had his testimony?"

Daniella paused her rifling about the jacket pocket.

She met my eye.

"We couldn't find him, Charlotte."

I felt my chest tighten, unable to quite believe what she was telling me. "You *lied* to me?"

Daniella glanced to the warden, as if I might get violent.

That felt like the largest betrayal of all . . . that, after all the time we'd spent together—after all the *time* we'd spent going through the documents—she believed I'd be capable of living up to my surroundings. Of turning some kind of untapped *aggression* upon her.

"I'm sorry, Charlotte," Daniella got out, standing up. "We couldn't let you in on all the information—I'm sure you understand."

She shifted towards the door, clearly intent on getting as far away from me as possible.

With her palm hovering over the red button which would

release her from my company, she seemed to catch something of her former resilience. She glanced back at me.

Gave me some doe-eyed pout of *sympathy*.

"I'm so sorry, Charlotte—*really*. We did all we could."

She hesitated another moment and then pounded the red button.

The door opened.

And she was gone.

A Decade Later

Freedom

The *drizzle soaked* my moleskin jacket as I walked the streets of Inverness.

A breeze was blowing down from the north. Frosty, cutting.

It felt as if there might be snow—or hail—sometime later.

When the day dawned.

I liked to walk through the deserted early-morning streets.

No crowds to navigate.

Nobody to speak with.

Alone with my thoughts.

Moving back home had been just as humiliating as I'd suspected it might be. My mother hadn't thought to pack up any of my room. She'd left all the posters from adolescent boy bands on the walls, the same ironic bedspread featuring thousands of fairies; made all the more ironic by the sordid acts I'd committed within their gaze.

My mother hadn't even packed away the clothes in the wardrobe.

All those same clothes which I'd fit into when I'd been twenty-one.

Strangely those same clothes weren't too small for me, by any means; actually, they were too large. I recalled trying on a woolly sweater I'd often use going out to meet with friends in the evenings—to the cinema; to the pub—and found that they *hung* off me . . . all baggy and clearly unusable for anything except lounging about the house, or amongst the very best of friends.

But, as I soon discovered, I didn't have any of those 'very best' friends.

Everybody, it seemed, had scarpered.

They'd been warned about my impending release so they could make themselves scarce.

I crossed over Ness Bridge, taking in Inverness castle.

A solitary Saltire unfurled in the quiet air.

I listened to the water stream by beneath the bridge, but didn't look.

Sometimes looking into the water would give me ideas . . . those same ideas, which, surely, were responsible for Eric taking his own life.

I strode on faster, tightening my grip on the messenger bag I'd taken out with me when I'd left my mum's house behind several minutes before. I had all that I needed for an overnight stay, and not much else. Money, of course, had been the biggest issue of all ever since my release from prison, but, as it turned out, my mother was only too happy to help out with that.

She had even arranged a bank account for me.

I supposed that since my father had left she had had more time to dedicate to her soon-to-return criminal daughter. Perhaps the state of my bedroom was simply a poorly executed display of affection. She had merely wanted me to feel like I had come home. That all my stuff was just as I had left it. That nothing had changed.

At Inverness Railway Station, I did battle with the ticket machine, finally getting it to spew out the return ticket to Edinburgh I'd need. The ticket would remain valid for a month, although I hoped that I'd have my business done well before then.

The train was predictably deserted.

Just the odd man or woman in a suit—bleary-eyed, yawning, clutching a disposable cup of coffee. Out of town for the day. Down to Edinburgh.

And back by night.

I passed the journey looking out of the window.

When we reached Aberdeen, I could take in the North Sea.

Strangely, despite the obviously frigid weather outside, the sight warmed me from within. I stared out over the uncompromising, inky-black waves and off to the horizon where I could make out dark clouds forming. Surely a storm coming later.

In Dundee, more people boarded the train.

I pulled my bag off the seat beside me and found myself surrounded on all sides by commuters. More people dressed in suits. Clutching briefcases. Rucksacks cradled in their laps.

And yet more cups of coffee.

The train arrived to Edinburgh just after nine, and I realised I had ample time to get my belongings together. My fellow passengers, the commuters, all seemed to be in an incurable hurry. They all bustled about, heading for the train doors. As if they craved escape from the carriage.

Soon afterwards, I joined them.

Since I didn't have a mobile phone of any description, I'd made a note of my destination in a simple notebook; also concealed within my messenger bag. I produced it, and then, realising that the address wasn't much help without a map, I plugged in the three pound coins which a nearby vending machine demanded. The machine spat out a pocket-sized city map into a metal tray.

With the map and the address in hand, I strode out of the station.

———

Since I hadn't the money for a taxi, I walked the entire route, folding up the map and then following the roads with my finger. As I went along, I heard my stomach rumbling. I had snatched a banana out of the fruit bowl before I'd left my mother's home, but that clearly hadn't been enough for the journey I'd planned. I handed over a crisp ten-pound note for a collection of cereal bars, a couple of sandwiches, and some bags of crisps. It all fit neatly into my messenger bag, making it bulge. Soon after I'd visited the shop—and eaten through a good proportion of my haul—I found the street.

Queen's Crescent.

I tossed the remains of my provisions into a nearby bin, and held the—now torn-free—page from my notebook tightly in my fist . . . as if I hadn't already memorised everything written on it. As if I wouldn't be seeing the house number in my dreams.

Number 64.

Eric's home—what had *been* Eric's home—turned out to be a terraced house. Its front garden consisted of concrete slabs. Some weeds grew in between the cracks. The front gate hung off a rusted-up hinge, and it creaked so loud that it seemed an almost moot point to ring the doorbell. I was sure that I would've been heard coming on in through the gate.

I waited on the front doorstep, feeling odd—out of place—to

be in this strange city, visiting a stranger out of the blue. I wondered how many people might wake up that morning *expecting* to find a *murderer* standing on their doorstep.

How many of those people on the train might've speculated that they would be sat beside a *murderer* when they bought their coffee?

And how many of those theoretical *murderers* might've been innocent . . . ?

I heard a brief scrabble from behind the door, and when the door did finally open up before me, the first thing I saw was the head of a black dog. It was a mongrel, perhaps a mix of a Labrador and some kind of sheepdog. It had grey hairs sprouting around its muzzle, and down its back. It seemed friendly enough, and—being the released murderer I was—I took kind greetings where I could.

The dog lolled its pink tongue out as it nuzzled the thigh of my jeans.

Only when I thought to glance up did I take note of the hesitant, nervous-looking face slipped in at the crack of the door.

My heart throbbed.

I took him in.

Eric's father.

I was most struck by how different he looked.

When he'd come to visit me in prison, he'd looked somewhat withered—*lanky*—but now he seemed positively *emaciated*. His cheeks looked almost as if they'd caved in. His eyes had become sunken in their sockets. His lips appeared almost *shrunken*.

He didn't recognise me, apparently.

I suppose my appearance had shifted somewhat too.

After I'd got out of prison, I'd grown my hair long.

And then there was the weight-loss issue.

"Mr Aldernaldy?" I said.

He blinked a couple of times. "Yes."

"Do you, uh . . . recognise me?"

He narrowed his eyes.

The wrinkles in his forehead made me wonder if he needed glasses but hadn't got around to getting his eyes checked. He gave a twitching shake of his head.

"Charlotte?" I said. "Charlotte Connolly?"

He continued to stare at me. He tilted his head to one side as if seeing me from a different angle might help with his comprehension of the situation.

"You came to see me, in prison? I was one of Eric's friends. We went together on the trip . . ."

And it was then that I saw something glint out from the back of his eyes.

He blinked again. He shifted back into the shadows of his home.

I thought he might call his dog back inside, and make to shut the door on me.

But, instead, he opened the door wide.

Grinning, the dog rounded my legs, and trotted back into the house.

Out of the frosted air.

"Please," Eric's father said. "Come in."

———

The house smelled of fly repellent and I soon saw why.

In the kitchen, roll upon roll of those gooey, honey-coloured strips hung down from the curtain rail. I saw many tiny black bodies stuck there.

Flies that'd perished.

From the looks of the sun-faded nature of the fly paper, I

could see that it'd been hanging for perhaps years in the same place.

The kitchen window looked out onto an overgrown garden. I could make out broken plant pots and a rusted-up rake among the long grasses.

"Tea?"

I turned back to Eric's father . . . to Patrick Aldernaldy.

As I took him in, I noticed he was trembling.

The dog arrived at his side, licked at his hand.

I did my best to smile although more than anything I wanted to cry.

Being here, being with Eric's father, it brought back all my memories of Eric.

How he had been kind-hearted . . . ready to joke around whenever the mood struck him.

In the wake of Petra's death it was easy to forget that.

It was easy to forget how all my 'friends' had appeared to change . . . or, perhaps, finally showed their real selves for the first time.

"Yes, please," I finally answered.

With a grunt, Eric's father clicked on a plastic kettle.

As it bubbled away, he leaned up against the kitchen counter. He fixed his stare on the floor tiles.

"I've come here to talk," I said. "Come to talk about Eric."

I don't know what I expected upon mentioning Eric's name.

Maybe I thought Eric's father would double over himself, break down in tears.

But he just kept on staring.

It *had* been ten years, I suppose . . .

The kettle boiled. Its switch clicked off.

At first, I thought Eric's father had missed this and I moved for the kettle, but, right at the last, Eric's father shifted from his position, mumbling something under his breath. From a cupboard, he produced a pair of chipped mugs, placed them on the kitchen counter.

He dumped a teabag in each cup and then poured in the boiling water.

His back was to me and I could hardly make out his words over the flow of the water.

"I was in prison once."

My heart skipped a beat. "Mr Aldernaldy?

He turned to me, looked over his shoulder. "Patrick," he said.

"*Patrick*," I said, taking the cup of tea he held out to me. "You were in prison?"

He brought his tea up to his lips, readying to take a sip. He paused. Blew across the surface. Then nodded.

Tail wagging, limping slightly, the dog shifted between us.

It sniffed about its food bowl set in the corner of the kitchen, and then, finding nothing but crumbs, turned its attention to the water beside it.

When I glanced back up at Patrick, I saw that he was looking down at the dog and smiling. "Sammy—she's my only company these days."

I looked back to the dog—*Sammy*.

She lapped at her water bowl.

I'd never had anything against dogs, or cats, but since I'd never grown up with either—my mother was always allergic—I'd never been able to relate to all those 'man's best friend' claims, or those ones about being a 'cat herder'. Maybe later, maybe now I was free—once I'd got a job—I'd find a place of my own and get a cat or dog . . . or both.

Patrick sipped at his tea. He gripped his mug tightly, stared down into its contents, then placed it on the kitchen counter. He smiled lightly at me, and I could see a sort of sharpness entering his eye. Something which seemed to have been somehow . . . *dimmed* ever since I'd got here.

"Eric never said? Never said about how he had a jailbird dad?"

I shook my head. "No, nothing."

"Mm," Patrick mumbled, glancing back down at Sammy. "'Struth."

A silence yawned wide before us.

I realised it was my turn to stoke the conversation.

"What did you do?" I said.

"Oh," Patrick said, "nothing . . . nothing *much*."

Despite everything—despite my weariness from the journey—a smile tugged at the corner of my mouth. "What?"

He breathed in deeply.

The way he breathed out suggested that he might've been a smoker once . . . it was in the way that he seemed to savour the gesture. "Assault," he said.

There might've been a time when I could've been caught off guard to know that I was in the same room with a violent convict. But not then.

He gave a profound sigh, then added, "Pub fight—pissed outta my skull, sure you know the deal, mm?"

He avoided my gaze for a long while, and when he finally did meet my eye, he looked somewhat sheepish. Almost like there was still a fifteen-year-old boy in there; ashamed of what he'd done. Worried about his mother's reprimands.

"Coupla years," he added. "Nothing like you."

We didn't say anything more about my crime.

It was thick between us in the air.

Once we'd finished our tea, the two of us seemed to be at a loose end. I became suddenly very conscious of the fact that I was awkwardly holding my messenger bag, clenching it tight across my stomach. "Mr, uh . . . *Patrick*—I was wondering if you could recommend me a B&B, somewhere close by?" I paused a beat, then added, "Somewhere *economical?*"

Having rinsed out the teacups, and set them to dry on the plastic rack, he looked to me, then said, "Got a spare room if it'll do you any good?"

I coloured a touch. "I wouldn't want to intrude."

"Intrude," he said, a slight smile appearing on his lips as he crouched down to pet Sammy's head. "Nah, it'll be a change to have some company, won't it, girl?"

———

Patrick set me up in the guest room.

I took in the slightly quaint surroundings.

Lacy white cloth was draped over the bedside table and the neat desk. There was a lamp and a telephone directory. The window was small. It looked out on the street. I supposed, since I'd been in such a rush—so *focussed* on the note—I hadn't previously had a proper chance to take in my surroundings. Now I saw that it was an attractive street. Lots of trees sprouted up from the pavements, their roots having cracked through the asphalt.

I set my messenger bag down on the chair at the desk.

Up here—*upstairs*—the smell of fly repellent wasn't so pronounced.

Because Patrick had told me to do so, I closed the door to the guest room and then lay down on the bed. I slept for several hours. And, by the time I'd got through, it was dark outside. I could hear the TV downstairs; chortling laughter, audience applause.

I shucked the bedsheets, realising I was still wearing my clothes from earlier in the day: a fleece over a t-shirt with a pair of jeans on underneath. I trudged to the bathroom to brush my teeth.

In the bathroom, I might've stumbled over the reason for Patrick's slightly dopey demeanour. I saw that a plastic bottle of painkillers had been left open. Apparently in a nosey mood, I pawed through the cabinet concealed behind the bathroom mirror and found many more bottles.

I'd made a point of steering clear of anything stronger than caffeine ever since I'd got out. The same way I'd made a point of doing my best to avoid bridges and other high places . . .

I descended the stairs.

Since the house wasn't too large—and because the TV was on so loud—it wasn't difficult to locate the living room, and Patrick. The only light in the living room came from the TV.

Patrick sat in an armchair, legs crossed.

Sammy, I saw, was slumped up against Patrick's legs.

Patrick's fingers lazily caressed her head.

I felt just a touch awkward, for the first time really clocking onto what it was I had done—what it was I was *doing*. But before I could attempt some sort of retreat, Patrick turned his head to me, smiled, then said, "Sleep well?"

"Fine, thanks," I said, taking a couple of tentative steps into the room.

On the TV, I saw the immaculately made-over presenters. For some reason, I'd thought that the tone they struck—the *pose*—suggested they were always talking down to their audience. As if they were addressing a roomful of nursery school children.

Perhaps a decade with hardly any TV had given me some much-needed distance.

"Take a seat," Patrick said.

I obeyed him, sinking down onto a sofa.

I glanced to Sammy whose sleepy eyes drifted over mine for a second before they turned back to the screen. For about ten minutes, we just sat there in silence, with the TV *babble* shouting all over us. When the gameshow, or whatever it was, wrapped up, Patrick produced the remote from somewhere and clicked the volume right down, rendering it a low-level chatter.

He looked to me, smiled, then said, "So, what brings you to Edinburgh, love?"

His eyes remained on me, that same, unplaceable, drifty expression lying over them.

That expression which, I supposed, was in part down to those pills in his bathroom.

My throat constricted.

Why *had* I come to Edinburgh?

Why *had* I turned up at what had once been Eric's home?

Why *was* I sitting in the living room with his father?

I hadn't really thought much of *why* . . . I'd thought so much of *why* while I'd been in prison that I suppose I'd pretty much tired myself out.

But I was a guest in Patrick's house.

And I owed him an explanation.

I looked to him, breathed in deep, and then said, "I wanted to know more about Eric—about *why* he . . . well, why he *did* what he did . . ."

Patrick's eyes seemed to sink back in their sockets.

It was surely the topic which he had been expecting all along.

What else rose the status of our relationship above strangers aside from the fact that I'd been friends with his son? That he'd come to visit me in prison?

Patrick turned his attention back to the TV.

For a moment I was sure he was going to turn the volume back up.

But his hands remained still.

It was as if he couldn't speak to me face to face . . . as if he *had* to address the TV . . . as if it was some sort of a coping mechanism. Then again, who was I to judge?

Nothing comparable had ever happened to me.

Nothing except spending a decent-sized portion of my youth behind bars.

Serving someone *else's* time.

"We weren't speaking much," Patrick said, to the TV. "But I knew he wasn't happy with something." He shook his head. "The way he'd come home, go up to his bedroom, and spend the entire weekend there. Never used to be like that," Patrick added, in a quieter voice.

I glanced down to Sammy, who I saw had perked her ears up, as if she understood every word. As if to salve her nerves, and not his own, Patrick gave her a scratch.

"He waited till I'd be out the house," Patrick went on. "Till he knew I'd be down the shops. Never would've gone if I'd known. Would've stayed. Would've talked him round. I know I would have."

In profile, I watched the single tear roll down Patrick's cheek.

It glinted in the TV light.

I waited out the pause, knowing that I'd no right to pry any further into this.

And yet there was one more question I needed to ask.

"Mr Aldernaldy, why did you come to the prison? Why didn't you just send some sort of correspondence, a letter? How did you even *know* where I was?"

Here Patrick turned away from the TV screen. He met my eye. Gave a slight smile . . . one of those smiles which—*I knew*—could give way to uncontrollable sobs at any moment.

"Left a note, Eric did." He sniffed, but this time it seemed to be a cold, rather than tears. "Told me that you were to know. Gave your details. Name, location, all that."

I managed to raise a flimsy smile by way of reply.

"Anything else?" I said.

Patrick shook his head, turned back to the TV screen, his outpouring of emotion—if that was what this had been—over. Sammy, too, turned her head back to the TV.

I eased myself up from the sofa, not wanting to intrude any further. Although I knew I should've been hungry, I couldn't quite face the prospect of eating. A rippling nausea had seized hold of my gut. As I stood in the doorway, I heard Patrick again.

"Charlotte?" he said. "You're welcome to stay just as long as you like—it's good to have company. If you'd like something to eat then there's some casseroles in the freezer, just gotta put them in the microwave for three minutes. That's all." He breathed heavily.

I readied to thank him, but he wasn't finished.

"And you'd be welcome to go and take a look in Eric's room . . . welcome to take anything you'd like from there. Everything's just how he left it . . . after he . . . after he *went*."

I stood there, in the doorway, for the longest time, not knowing what to say.

How was I supposed to know *what* to say?

In the end, I just settled on a simple, "Thank you," and headed up to Eric's bedroom.

A Cry For Help

Perhaps *I expected* Eric's bedroom to be locked, or for there to be a police cordon around it to stop careless passers-by—like myself—from trespassing on the scene.

But, as it happened, there was nothing—nothing at all.

All I had to do was turn the doorknob and I was inside.

The first thing I noted was the childlike cut-out wooden letters on the door which spelled out 'ERIC' in multi-coloured block capitals. Each of the letters featured an animal . . . an elephant for the 'E', a rabbit for the 'R', an insect for the 'I', then, finally, a cat for the 'C'.

Strangely, seeing those letters tickled something within me.

Something deep down in my chest.

I felt a warmth in the corners of my eyes.

But I carried on, stepped into what had been Eric's bedroom.

True to Patrick's word, Eric's bedroom appeared to have been preserved just as it had been before he died. The bedroom itself belied the childish wooden letters stuck onto the door.

The bed was made. A neutral, patterned blue duvet covered

it. The pillows had been plumped up, as if Eric might return at any moment, looking for a decent night's rest.

The walls were mostly bare. They featured only a poster of the Hearts football squad and then an assortment of yellow sticky notes by the desk. I examined the notes around the desk more closely.

Nothing I could make sense of . . . mostly just to-do items, shopping lists and the names and numbers of various people.

The blind was drawn down over the window as if sunlight might adversely affect the museum-like, preserved quality of Eric's bedroom.

A computer sat up on the desk.

I checked it over, saw that it was still plugged into the wall.

Although Patrick had clearly given me permission to do whatever I wanted in Eric's room, I couldn't help but glance back over my shoulder. For some reason, I expected to find Sammy there, looking in on me. But there was no dog. And no sign of Patrick.

I turned back to the computer.

Tapped the Power switch.

The computer was an old model, even for ten years ago, and I heard the cooling fans clinking and clanking away within the tower. I perched on the desk chair, wary of not wanting to become too comfortable. I wanted to be able to shift away from the screen at a moment's notice.

Patrick might've given me permission to do whatever I wished in Eric's bedroom, but that didn't mean I wanted him to see me browsing through the files on his son's computer.

As Eric had been in life, so was his computer in death.

Once I'd closed down the barrage of messages asking me to update software, I took in the screen.

His desktop background was an emerald hue . . . not that I could make much of it out for the sea of icons which dotted the entire screen. I perused them all, moving down one column, and then the next. I don't know quite what I was looking for. Perhaps I wanted a folder labelled something along the lines of 'Petra's murder', but, if that was the case, then I was doomed to be disappointed.

I sank back on the desk chair, losing my earlier caution.

I thought about digging through the contents of Eric's hard drive, of having to go through all the documents, seeing if there was anything which fit—what did that even *mean?*—but I decided it better to resist. I could've been there for days systematically going through all of Eric's files, and, at the back of my mind, I didn't want to intrude on his privacy—which was to say his *memory*—by uncovering something which might warp my opinion of him.

I had decided to shut down the computer, and go looking for the casseroles which Patrick had so kindly offered me, when I thought of one more thing.

I clicked the icon for his internet browser.

The screen immediately filled with a blinding grey-white window.

I shielded my eyes from the sight.

I hadn't thought to switch on the main light of Eric's bedroom.

I was depending on the light from out on the landing.

The internet browser asked me to update it and I politely declined.

I found the option to look at the browsing history and clicked it.

. . . And was *overwhelmed* with results.

If the task of pawing through Eric's hard drive for clues as to Petra's murder had been something this side of crazy, then, well, I can't think to describe what *this* might be . . .

There were websites of all sorts.

Many based on climatic and meteorological research. Those had been Eric's areas of speciality. I supposed he had managed to find a job in either of those fields.

Was work what had weighed Eric down?

I scrolled through them all, noting many of them for myself —many resources which I'd used for research while writing assignments for university.

For my unfinished degree in geography . . .

Finally I found something. A news article.

I clicked it.

THE LOCH MONAR KILLER

Although I read the words of the article, none of them really sank into my brain.

It was impossible to square the names written there with real life. To see the names of my 'friends' written out in the text . . . and the details of those *bizarre* days all being sketched out in a cold, unfeeling *factual* style. I left that article behind, selected another in Eric's history.

LOCH MONAR KILLER GETS LIFE

The article, this time, had a large picture.

A picture from the fieldtrip.

A picture of *me*.

I could tell, from my complexion—from my *grin*—that I was drunk.

I wondered if it'd been taken on the night of Petra's murder.

The picture was slightly blurred.

I hardly recognised the girl staring out at me.

Again, I didn't dwell too long on the article, knowing that it would only be a rabbit hole. That I could—quite easily—lose several hours to all of these second-hand impressions, all these 'expert' opinions. I returned to Eric's history, seeing that there was a forum specified there.

A forum, not particularly tactfully named, BRIDGE-JUMPERS ANON.

I clicked it.

Straightaway, I deduced which was Eric's profile, the—again —not particularly tactfully named HeartsTilAyeDie.

I selected his messaging history.

Got down into all the chats he'd been having.

I started with his oldest posts first.

What surprised me the most, I suppose, was that, throughout all of his messages back and forth with other members, he took on the role of the voice of reason . . . the one who was constantly handing out tips, sparked with humour, on how to cope with their tendencies.

As I reeled through Eric's messages, I expected to find a gradual shift in tone, to see him become the person asking for help . . . the one asking after support . . . but, again, that wasn't the case.

Not until his final post.

The one marked out as 'My Last Day'.

I read it from start to finish:

So, from the title, I'm sure you can deduce the intent of this message. And if you can't, well, don't kill yourself over it(!).

Nah, I've decided that this is it . . . although I haven't spoken much about it here I've been thinking about 'it' for months. Now's the time. Hanging, I reckon. Or maybe some pills. I'll see how I feel.

As for some parting words of wisdom, how about, 'Do the right thing—always. Or else it'll haunt you forever.'

Ciao

HTID

I stared on at the message.

Tried to get it through my brain.

But, no matter how hard I tried, I just couldn't.

I knew that there had to be more to the story.

When I checked on the time difference between his final message, and his penultimate one—one in which he had suggested the sufferer get professional help—there was only two hours.

Something had happened in those two hours which'd changed Eric's mind . . . well, something which'd shifted him off the track of tentatively *thinking* about suicide to actually pulling it off. I thought back to my own, admittedly limited, experience with suicide, and couldn't help wondering if I hadn't heard from somewhere—from *someone*—that a suicide attempt was often a cry for help . . . that those who eventually went through with the act did so after many times trying . . .

But Eric had found the guts—if that was the right way to put it—straight away.

He had made no mistake.

I leaned back in the desk chair.

Downstairs I could hear the loud *babble* of the TV.

Outside, in the street, I listened to a car pass by.

I turned my attention back to the screen, not really looking for anything in particular.

And that was when I noticed the icon.

Blinking at me.

NEW MESSAGES!

———

If I'd had any scruples about digging through my dead friend's personal life, I certainly didn't have them now. I clicked on the icon, waited for the browser to load, and was taken off guard to find myself—*right away*—staring at Eric's inbox.

Obviously there were thousands of unread messages.

Pages and pages and *pages* of them.

I wondered at what point the email provider would think of deleting his account.

They hadn't got around to it yet . . . and I had to admit I was glad.

I scrolled through the pages and pages of newsletters, and emailed reminders—there were even some birthday greetings from distant relatives or friends who, apparently, hadn't heard the news.

When I got to the read emails, I scrolled my way to the top.

To the last email Eric had read before he died.

There was no subject line.

And I could, already, see who the sender was:

Graeme Neal.

My blood ran cold.

My heart rapped against my ribs . . . my muscles all seized tight.

But I held my nerve and clicked on the email.

The first of the messages was from Eric to Graeme:

Hey,

I know we're meeting up today, in town, and I know you said that we weren't to speak about the plan like this. But I wanted to let you know about the decision I've taken, that I'm not going to stick to the arrangement any longer. Charlie doesn't deserve this. Nobody *deserves this. I think it's time the truth came out. It's been long enough.*

Fair warning.

Rick

Somehow, even though now it meant nothing—even though I'd lost my twenties over this—I couldn't help but feel a weight lifting off my shoulders.

Here it was—here it *was*—proof that I wasn't crazy.

That I'd been innocent all along.

My eyes wandered down to the next message.

The reply from Graeme:

Talk later,

G

Even now—even through the veil of ten years gone by—I couldn't help but wince at the fact that I'd *ever* found Graeme attractive. I remembered how his nickname used to be 'G', and that he'd insist everyone refer to him that way.

For some reason, over time, I've learned not to take people seriously when they go by a single initial . . . I guess I always was a slow learner.

And here it was.

I'd found the killer.

Eric's killer.

It had been just as I'd thought.

Eric *hadn't* committed suicide.

I flipped back to BRIDGE-JUMPERS ANON.

I looked a little more closely at Eric's final message.

The one I'd read posted there.

Had he really been the one to write that?

———

When I peeled my eyes away from the computer monitor, when I made to shut it down, I wondered if I should print off what I'd discovered . . . the email, and that posting to the forum. It was like a splash of cold water across my face to think that this meant nothing now; that—*surely*—this wasn't enough to prove anything.

And where even *was* Graeme these days?

Might he have a family, kids?

Might they *all* have families and kids?

Mercy and Alex, too?

It was a somewhat macabre thought to reflect on the fact that, of the six of us that'd set out on the fieldtrip, only four of us were still alive . . . as far as I knew.

I felt a strange fizzing sensation through my bloodstream.

I have no way of knowing how long I sat there.

How long I stared into the eyes of each and every member of the Hearts football team in the poster of the squad on the wall.

I think it was when I heard the *drawl* of the TV suddenly come to an end that I eventually shifted up off the desk chair, crossed Eric's room, and headed out into the corridor.

Closing Eric's bedroom door behind me.

I listened to the *zip* of Patrick's slippers treading over the carpet downstairs.

Slowly I made my way down the steps.

My breathing came short and insufficient.

A couple of times, I almost tripped.

Tumbled all the way down.

I clung to the banister for balance.

When I reached the bottom of the staircase it was somehow one of the great achievements; on the same page as climbing Everest or walking on the moon.

I steadied myself and then walked into the kitchen.

Patrick was in the process of filling a hot water bottle with the kettle.

As the steam rose up, it set Patrick in a kind of ghostly light.

Sammy, I saw, had curled up in her wicker basket beneath the kitchen counter.

Patrick finally noticed me, turned.

Smiled.

"Didn't fancy casserole, then?" he said, his tone a touch jovial.

I tried to smile along, but since I knew the gravity of what was to come—what I was going to have to ask—I couldn't make much of a fist of it. "Patrick?" I said.

He continued to fill the hot water bottle.

He screwed the cap onto the hot water bottle then turned to me.

"I was just wondering," I continued, "if, when . . . I mean, *how* you came across Eric."

I studied his face, wondering how he might react.

His eyes seemed to go distant, but there were no tears this time.

"It was quiet," he said, "*really* quiet—I think that was how I knew." He glanced to me. "I mean, when I walked in through the front door, the house just felt *different*."

I looked back into his eyes.

I sensed that Sammy was watching this conversation from her wicker basket.

Somehow understanding *everything*.

"I had the shopping," he went on, "and I left it in the hall. Something told me . . . it just *told* me that I had to go upstairs; that I had to go and check on Eric—see what was wrong."

Here Patrick switched to staring at the kitchen wall.

"At first I thought he'd gone out. I called out his name, waited for a reply, but"—he shook his head—"nothing back. Unlike him. Even if it was just a mumble, he always answered."

I felt my gut dip.

My heart beat faster.

"His bedroom door was left just a little ajar. I remember thinking that it was further closed than normal . . . that it wasn't usually like that . . . I suppose that was when I knew there was something seriously wrong, you know?"

I looked past Patrick, out into the garden.

There was something which I hadn't seen before, but which was prevalent in the moonlight. A climbing frame and slide. Like everything else in the garden, it was nearly buried by the long grasses. No wonder I'd missed it first time I'd looked.

Patrick continued, "When I pushed the door, there was this . . . this *dead* weight." Here something caught in his throat. "But I kept on pushing—*pushing* as hard as I could manage . . . it seemed important that I get the door open. It was around that point, when I'd just managed to budge the door open just enough to squeeze around that I noticed Sammy—she'd clambered her way up the stairs. She was sticking her nose in through the crack. She knew there was something wrong."

"And?" I said, only catching myself, feeling that I was being insensitive, a beat or so later . . . and by then it was far too late to think about stuff like that.

175

"I got in around the doorframe, and I saw his body . . . *Eric's* body . . ." Patrick illustrated with his hands, making to tie a noose. "He'd strung himself up on the back of the door—from the doorknob."

There was a long pause in the kitchen.

The air seemed so charged, as if one of us had only to strike a match to set a swirling inferno blazing through the house.

I held myself very still, knowing that I had to tread *very* carefully. And then, because I could find no other way to go, I said, "Did the police find anything suspicious—any sign of *foul* play?"

For the first time, Patrick looked at me with anything other than kindness.

Actually, thinking back, it was *anger*.

And perhaps not without reason . . .

"Just what're you insinuating?" he said. "That *I* murdered him? My own *boy*?"

His voice was gruff, and just below the level of a shout.

I knew that the walls between these houses were paper-thin.

And that it wouldn't take much to get somebody calling the police.

For someone like me—somebody who wasn't long out of prison; and serving for a crime as serious as the one I had been—that wouldn't be best advised.

"Nothing then?" I said, purposely trying to lower my tone.

To sound *calmer*.

It seemed to work—Patrick seemed to reel himself in.

Perhaps the effect of his painkillers was wearing off.

"No," Patrick said. "They said it was a standard case. Found some note on a message board telling others he would do it. He left that note, telling me to tell you, and saying where you were holed up." He blew out a sigh, and his body seemed to deflate. "No 'rough edges' I believe is the way they put it."

" 'No rough edges'."

Patrick breathed in deeply as if attempting to restore himself to his former stature.

He glanced down at Sammy, smiled, apparently having forgotten about my insinuation.

"Poor, old girl," he said, "she used to sleep on the foot of my bed, but she doesn't get herself much up the stairs these days." He yawned. "All right," he said, his hot water bottle clasped down at his thigh, "I'm turning in—make yourself at home: telly, fridge, freezer, take whatever it is you want. Stay as long as you want."

As he passed by me, he laid a reassuring hand on my shoulder, then squeezed gently.

I listened to his footsteps as he headed up the staircase, to bed.

When I turned my attention to the kitchen, feeling my stomach grumbling away from hunger, I glanced over to Sammy and wished—more than anything—that she might be able to talk.

Somehow, I figured that she might have something interesting to say about what she saw . . . if she could speak. If she hadn't been a dog.

Scot-Free

I*n the morning*, I did everything I had to do as quickly as I could manage.

When I woke up, opened the door of the guest room, I found a towel awaiting me. I assumed, from the towel, that I was permitted to use the soap and shampoo in the bathroom. It felt good to get myself shot of all the smells of my journey. And, when I emerged, through the warm steam, I felt almost like a new woman.

Once I'd got myself dressed in fresh clothes I almost felt *positive* about the whole thing.

. . . There was only the small matter of the murderer to track down . . .

I used Eric's computer again in the morning, doing a search for Graeme, Mercy and Alex, hoping to find some details on their whereabouts. I found out, almost straightaway, that Alex was in Edinburgh . . . Mercy and Graeme were down south. As far as I was able to tell from various social media, the two of them were in the London area.

Alex had been so kind as to post his address for anybody to see.

Mercy and Graeme would be a larger step for me, and it would certainly stretch my funds. So it would be Alex who I'd go to first.

I told Patrick that I was going out to see some friends.

From his spot in front of the TV, he only smiled back at me, his eyes again seeming to be swimming beneath some invisible sea.

I walked along the grassy valley beneath the castle. Warm, blue skies soared above and it was wonderful to feel the warmth of the sun's rays on my back. I recalled having seen the odd prison film or two, and wondering about how, once they got out —as they almost inevitably did—they would go somewhat crazy in their new surroundings.

To be reconnected to nature.

But now I truly understood.

And, never again, would I take the Great Outdoors for granted.

Alex's street was wide and filled with large houses; the sorts of houses which, I knew, would number into the range of millions of pounds. From the looks of the cars parked up on the street, there wasn't any little neighbourly competition, either.

It seemed as though Alex had truly entered into the spirit of the human *race*.

Objectively speaking, his house was the very largest on the street, and there was a pair of brand-new four-by-fours parked up in the driveway. Both cars had tinted windows in the back. Nothing says luxury—nothing says *rich*—like privacy.

Feeling out of place, I picked my way over the round marble slabs set into the chalky-grey gravel drive and stood on the doorstep. I took a moment to collect myself, wondering if I should've phoned ahead. But I'd thought that would just give Alex a chance to evade me.

He could hardly evade me when I was *right* here.

I reached up and rang the bell.

A doleful, flat note sounded about the—apparently—sizeable interior.

Somehow, perhaps because of the build-up, what I most expected was to be greeted by a housemaid dressed in a black-and-white uniform.

What I *didn't* expect, however, was to find myself standing nose to nose with Alex himself.

He wore an over-washed, roll-neck jumper with fuzzy motes hanging off it.

Underneath, he wore a pair of cream trousers with a sharp crease pressed into them.

I couldn't help but note how *mature* of an image Alex struck.

Standing the two of us together, back to back, I wondered if anyone would be able to tell that the two of us were the same age.

From behind a pair of large-lensed glasses, he cocked his head to one side. "Good morning?" he said. "How can I help?"

"Don't you recognise me, Alex?"

He squinted at me.

Then he seemed to lean back into his house, as if I might have some contagious disease.

His eyes widened.

He spoke quickly and in a tone which suggested he wasn't accustomed to being flustered—as he apparently was now.

"Please," he said, "come inside."

———

Alex's house was just as grand within as it was out.

A pair of entwining marble staircases were the prominent feature of the hall.

Then there were the chandeliers.

The many flowers all propped up on stands.

Even despite the situation, how I'd so obviously thrown Alex, I couldn't help but mutter, "Almost like the Amazon in here."

Alex glanced back at me briefly. "My wife *likes* flowers," he replied.

I couldn't help but note the slightly bitter tone to his voice.

To how he talked about his wife.

I wondered what Petra might've made of his wife . . .

Alex led me through a neat series of corridors into what seemed to me to be a subsidiary conservatory. If his wife 'liked' flowers as much as Alex claimed then I supposed there would be a much larger one somewhere else about the house.

Petunias, creeping vines and an out-of-control rubber plant were those which most immediately struck me . . . the plants which I *immediately* recognised.

Alex wagged a hand to indicate one of the white wicker armchairs. "Sit, please."

Still somewhat taken aback by my surroundings—by how Alex had landed on his feet—I'm sure I resembled something of a startled deer.

Once I'd sat down, Alex perched on the armchair opposite me, then said, "What do you want?"

"Well, Alex," I replied, with a slight smile. "It's nice to see you, too."

"Don't you have a . . . a . . ." He flapped a hand about his head as if this cleared everything up.

"You mean, they let me go?" I said. "That I'm a free woman once again?"

"Uh-huh," he replied, through gritted teeth.

I glanced about me. "You've done well for yourself."

"Yes, yes," he said. "Mapping software . . . lots of room for manoeuvre these days." He flashed me a smile which, if it was meant to be reassuring, fell flat on its face.

I looked out of the conservatory, into the garden. "Where's your wife?"

"On holiday," he said, drumming his fingers on the armrest of his chair. "In the Caribbean. She doesn't *enjoy* Scottish winters," he added, as if it mattered.

I turned back to Alex.

Looked him in the eye.

I couldn't quite shift the slightly naughty pleasure I got from toying with him.

I'd never had the chance to make someone so uncomfortable from my mere *presence* before.

"They didn't tell you I'd be getting out?" I said.

He shook his head. "No, why would they tell me that?"

I shrugged. "I thought you and Mercy—*Graeme*—talked an awful lot."

"No, no, that's not right. We haven't spoken since . . ."

I allowed his reply to hang in the air.

Waiting for him to fill in the gaps.

But he held himself still.

I noticed that his leg was jiggling—that he was bouncing with nervous energy.

"You heard about Eric, then?" I said.

Alex rolled his eyes back. "Of course," he replied. "That was such a long time ago now . . . it seems like another *life*, really."

I picked up on that.

Wondered how he saw that fateful fieldtrip. How he saw *me* . . . was that the truth, that I was just some uncomfortable reminder of a life that he would rather forget? What else did I expect?

Alex turned his attention back onto me. "Charlotte," he said, his tone more reasonable now—I wondered if this was the sort of tone he might strike with one of his clients. "What do you *want*?"

I breathed in the heavy scent of the conservatory.

The overpowering odour of the plants.

It was like my wildest dreams.

"I want to know the truth," I said. "I want *justice*."

Alex held himself still. " 'Justice' ?" he said. "*Justice* was done —justice was you going to prison for what you did. Justice was—"

I held up my hand.

Shook my head.

"Alex, please, we both know that's not true. No matter how much you've tried to convince yourself of that story, we know that's simply *not* what happened."

Alex went quiet now.

Apparently accepting this.

I wondered if I could really blame him . . . the most probable thing was that he *had*, on some level, allowed himself to believe their invented version of events.

Self-deception is a pitiable thing.

When Alex spoke again, his voice was a broken whisper. "What do you want, after all these years? What do you want us to *do*?"

That, I supposed, was the closest I was going to get to an apology.

I'd have to take it for now.

"What happened that day, Alex? Why won't anybody tell the truth? You all tried to convince me that I pushed Petra into killing herself . . . and then the lot of you stitched me up; made it seem like I was *actually* the one with the weapon." I shook my head. "I know about Eric—that he was ready to help out with my appeal, that he was going to tell the truth after all."

Alex pressed his lips tightly together, squeezing all the blood out of them.

He met my eye for a second then looked away.

I went on. "I've been through all of the information—all of the interviews, Alex. There're inconsistencies in the stories, all over the place . . ."

But Alex wasn't listening to me. He was drumming his fingers hard against the armrest and staring out into the garden. I hoped he had turned his mind back to that day—to the day when we'd discovered Petra's body. Some deep, dark, part of me very much hoped that he was suffering, and that he would *continue* to suffer, all over again.

Perhaps, in his own way, he'd served his own punishment.

Finally, Alex glanced up. He stared back into my eyes. I saw, all of a sudden, a frightened boy staring out at me. No older than twenty-one years old. Everything surrounding him—the house, the luxuries—was merely a façade. He wished, more than anything, that what'd already happened in his past might be forgotten. It surprised me when he was the one to shatter the silence.

"Where're you staying?" he said. "In town?"

I nodded. "With Eric's dad."

" 'Eric's dad' ?" Alex said, arching an eyebrow.

I wondered how this could possibly be pertinent information for him.

Feeling as though my welcome was well and truly worn out, I rose to my feet.

And Alex, apparently sensing the same, got to his feet too.

"Well," I said, with a fake smile. "It was nice to see you after all these years. I'll leave you in peace now, I'm sure you've got things to do."

Alex nodded in agreement, but he wouldn't meet my eye.

He led me back out through the house.

Each step closer to the door, I sensed a lifting of the tension which loomed over the pair of us. It was the strangest thing. There was almost a skip in Alex's step.

As he rested his thumb on the door latch, he was positively beaming. "So," he said, "hope you enjoy your stay in Edinburgh —heading back up to Inverness soon, are you?"

I shook my head. "Actually, I was thinking about heading down to London, to go pay Mercy and Graeme a visit."

The muscles in Alex's forearm tensed. He held the door stiffly. "Why would you want to do that?"

"Like I said, I want to know the truth—I want to know what happened that day."

"And then?" he replied, rapid-fire.

"Don't know, guess I'll cross that bridge when I come to it."

I glanced to the front door, and to the day outside.

It was overcast; a grisly grey.

For the first time in our meeting, I actually wanted to get away from Alex.

"Charlotte," Alex said, paused, then corrected himself, "*Charlie*; isn't there anything I can say that'll make you leave the past alone? Some things are just best forgotten . . . some things are just best swept under the rug, so to speak. Do you follow?"

I looked into Alex's eyes, seeing the fear.

I couldn't help feeling that Alex knew what'd happened. That he'd known about Graeme . . . and how he'd *killed* Eric before covering it up—making it look like suicide . . .

Did he think I was in danger?

Was there some *authentic* willingness for me not to come to harm?

I didn't think it likely.

As far as Alex was concerned—as far as *any of them* were concerned—everything would be neatly wrapped up, brought to an end, if I was to tumble underneath a passing lorry.

But I was determined not to allow that to happen.

Not before I'd solved this thing, in any case.

"See you, Alex," I said, and then turned my attention back to the door.

After a brief pause, Alex swung the door open, allowing me to leave.

I flashed a smile and then strode out past him.

What he couldn't see was how quickly my heart was beating.

Or how I'd been considering anything in close range—an umbrella in the hat stand—as a weapon I might use in self-defence.

Down South

I *thought of something* I might be able to leave Patrick as a token of thanks for unexpectedly putting me up for the night. But I couldn't find anything appropriate in the corner shop, and the only other shop I ran into on the way back to his house was filled with tourist junk.

When I got back to the house, it was much like when I'd arrived. Sammy nuzzled at my jeans, her bedraggled tail batting away furiously, making little snorts of excitement. Once she'd hobbled away, into the house, I found myself standing before Patrick.

"Heading off, are you?"

I looked back into his eyes. "How did you know?"

"Just a gut feeling."

Patrick turned into the house, going after Sammy.

I followed.

It didn't take me long to pack everything away. Since it took me less than a minute to get everything ready, I was certain that

I'd missed something. That I'd left something behind. But, in the end, I convinced myself it was because I'd packed *extremely* light.

Only when I glanced up did I realise that Patrick was standing in the doorway to the guest room. That he was leaning against the doorframe.

He seemed almost to be looking right through me.

To something on the other side.

All the same, I smiled at him.

And he smiled back.

"It's been nice having you to stay," he said. "Nice to have some company about the place." He paused, drew a breath and then sighed it out. "Gets awfully lonely here, sometimes."

Although it seemed impertinent to me at the time, I couldn't help but ask the question. "What about Eric's mum?" I said. "Is she not around?"

Patrick shook his head. "Nah, no, she's not . . ."

From the hurt—*weathered*—tone of his voice, I decided not to ask a follow-up question; to determine whether it was because she'd died or because she'd left.

On my way out of the house, down in the front hall, I acted on instinct when Patrick stretched out his hand for me to give a shake. I lurched forwards and embraced him, squeezing him tightly. And although he didn't throw his arms about me in return, I could tell, from the way his body relaxed—the way his shoulders slumped—that he was glad for the gesture. I wondered how long it'd been since he'd felt the touch of another human being.

The last time he scooped change into a cashier's palm?

I said goodbye to Sammy, too, who seemed to recognise the gentle note of sadness in the air. Her ears dipped a little although her tail continued to wag weakly. I supposed, in her doggy brain, she recalled all the times that Eric had left the house, only to return weeks, or months, later.

Perhaps, as far as I knew, Sammy understood that I would *never* return.

Since it took me about half the time to reach the station than it had from the station to Patrick's house, I reached the conclusion that I'd taken a wrong turn on my arrival.

A train was leaving for London in an hour or so.

I visited the cash machine, took out a hundred pounds. I bought another return ticket, this time from Edinburgh to London. When I caught a glimpse of the price I wondered if I wouldn't have been better off flying. But, then again, I wasn't in any hurry.

It wasn't like the past was going to change while I sat on a train for eight hours or so.

I got myself a coffee and a cheese sandwich, then I sat on the platform and watched the trains coming and going. It was somewhat calming to feel the gentle, cool breeze blowing through the station building; to breathe in the scent of grease and steam. From within my messenger bag, I dug out a scarf and wrapped it about my neck.

It sent a warming tickle through my blood to feel the woolly material against my skin.

The train was direct, although it stopped a half dozen times.

I noted my progress as I went along; passing through Newcastle, York, Peterborough.

Then down to London.

Back when I'd been younger, I'd often taken trips with my family down south. One of my aunts had lived in Essex, and we would go there to spend the week at their large house. We used to do that once a year until my aunt moved to Australia. Then the trips down south came to a stop. The only times when I ventured much out of Inverness was for geography fieldtrips. Getting about the country, as a student, wasn't the cheapest of propositions.

The train slunk into King's Cross just after night fell. As I eyed the buildings all springing up at either side of the tracks, I couldn't help but feel a touch intimidated.

I'd only visited London a handful of times; and those times had been carefully orchestrated expeditions. There had always been clear goals in mind.

To go to *Madame Tussauds* or else the *British Museum*.

And this time, I suppose, I had just as clear of a goal as before.

I was going to find out what happened at Loch Monar.

I decided to find a hostel to stay at for the night, and, with the help of a member of the King's Cross Station staff, I picked out a place just around the corner. It was bristling with a myriad of accents and languages. The front hall was stuffed full with battle-hardened backpacks. I waded my way through to the front desk, and got myself a bed in one of the dormitories.

I'd like to say that it was a well-earned night's rest, but it was almost impossible to get more than a few minutes' sleep at a time what with the constant comings and goings; the way that the door to the dormitory seemed to swing open all the time.

The sound of suitcase wheels across the floor.

I was glad when I noted the dawning day creeping in around the decrepit curtains of the dormitory, and I grabbed my messenger bag—lying in my bunk beside me—sneaking out to the bathrooms for a quick shower before the day ahead.

Soon after, I got down to some more research using the free internet in the front hall of the hostel. I browsed through those same social media sites, digging out yet more information on Graeme and Mercy. I'd decided that I would leave Graeme for last . . . perhaps it was a simple desire for a dramatic finale, or maybe I was a touch afraid.

Mercy had been kind enough to post a personal CV listing all of the companies she'd worked for, including the current organisation: Camden Council. I could see, from the information she'd voluntarily shared, that she was currently on the planning committee.

I supposed she'd put her geography degree from the University of Inverness to good use . . . just as Alex had done.

Again, perhaps with too much of a flare for drama, I planned to lurk near her offices and ambush her sometime around lunch. She was close to the hostel—only around the corner, in fact.

Before going on stake-out, I dug through a nearby second-hand bookshop and bought a few tatty paperbacks to keep me entertained throughout the morning. Next, I bought a half dozen bananas and a few pots of yoghurt. My more or less healthy breakfast habits surprised even me.

I found a park opposite Mercy's offices, and I picked out the least-rickety looking, and least bird-poo-splattered bench. I was lucky. That time in the morning there weren't many tourists.

Throughout the morning, I was dimly aware of the park filling more and more; the chattering groups filling up the space surrounding me. Over the top of my book, I glanced to the doorway of Mercy's office building. Every so often, I would see someone, dressed in a suit—usually with a briefcase, or a businesslike handbag—come trudging out. They would, almost without exception, take a glance at their wristwatch or else slip their phone out from their pocket.

Apparently running against a clock.

It was just before midday when people began to pour out of the entranceway of the office building. I left my bench behind. A young Japanese couple quickly took up the vacated spot.

I hustled through the crowds on the pavements, getting myself closer to the entranceway of the office building. I eyed the people, already realising how many of them there were—and that it would be so easy for someone I had last seen over a *decade* ago to disappear amongst them.

But, even if I didn't catch her today, there was always tomorrow.

I was determined to track Mercy down.

Even if it took the rest of the week.

Or the rest of my life.

I raised my shoe up onto a low concrete wall and feigned tying my shoelace while I kept up an eye on the exodus. I might well have missed her, among the group of girls; all of them wearing skirts which arrived just above the knee. If she hadn't turned her head, glanced in my direction, then I might well have done. As it was, though, my eyes passed over her and I knew that I had found her . . . those hamster-like cheeks hadn't changed at all.

Not even after ten years.

Her hair, though, was no longer a mousy brown.

She'd dyed it that edgy-red colour which seemed so in fashion.

I finished up with my fake shoelace-tying and perused the group of girls. The group of seven or eight soon divided into pairs, and a trio . . . Mercy a part of the latter. While the pairs of girls crossed the road, headed for the park where I'd been sat, I kept on the tail of Mercy's trio.

Mercy, of course, was in the middle of them.

As I closed on their heels, I tried to make out what they were saying, but it was impossible to understand anything meaningful above the babbling voices which filled the air.

Mercy and her companions turned off the main road and down a side alley.

I kept pace with them, feeling my heart throbbing in my throat.

Although I knew what I was doing was *legal*, I couldn't quite get my head around the fact that I wasn't doing something wrong. It felt as if I was crossing a line. As if I should slip back into the shadows. Return to my bedroom in my mum's house. Forget any of this had happened.

It was the same feeling I'd had when I'd approached Alex's house.

Like I was just a nuisance . . .

But it was one thing to be a nuisance, and quite another to be a *wronged* nuisance.

I would put that right, though.

Mercy's companions suddenly bent into her, both delivered a pair of pecks on either of her cheeks, and they headed off in another direction.

This was it.

This was my opportunity.

I waited till the girls were out of earshot, and then I called Mercy's name.

She halted.

Turned.

Saw me.

Ran.

———

I hardly got my head around what'd just happened.

I delayed getting one foot in front of the other for several moments, and, in that time, Mercy almost managed to get away from me. She did manage to get a head-start.

But I wasn't slow.

Prison food had at least had the positive side-effect that it'd encouraged me to stay slim.

To stay fighting fit.

Ready for a race when one cropped up.

I pumped my legs, feeling the pavement beneath the soles of my trainers.

My heart beat harder.

I caught sight of Mercy's red hair as she turned the corner.

Into the street beyond.

I heard the *screech* of brakes.

I caught up . . . just in time to see Mercy dancing between a pair of cars.

Before the cars could pull out again, I twisted between them.

Someone honked their horn.

Mercy disappeared into an alleyway. She ran on harder.

Already, though, I could see her mistake. A dead-end.

As if she'd only just realised it herself, she glanced back over her shoulder at me.

I wondered if she was going to cry out for help.

If she was going to find a policeman to arrest this *nasty* girl chasing her.

It would only take the theoretical policeman the best part of a minute to run a check on my name. To find out just which crime was attached to my name. If Mercy wanted to keep running—if Mercy *really* wanted to keep running—then she could easily do so.

But her frightened, startled-doe eyes fixed onto me. I think she realised that she could run today, but I would find her tomorrow.

I wouldn't be stopped forever.

I took steps towards her, hearing a puddle splash beneath the tread of my trainers. As with all alleyways, it smelled unpleasant; that sickly sweet odour of rotting rubbish.

When I'd got close enough, I said, "It's nice to see you too, Mercy."

Mercy's lips latched open but she made no sound.

I waited . . . waited for her to get her act together . . . and then, finally, she replied.

"How . . . how did you find me?"

I smirked. "Wouldn't you like to know."

"I *would* actually."

There was the snippy tone from before. The one which I had always associated with Mercy.

I shrugged, not seeing any reason to hide it. "Online—you should probably take greater care with the stuff you put out in public, especially when you're trying *not* to be found."

She seemed to have nothing to add to this.

A slight smile appeared on her lips.

She took a confident step forwards.

Into me.

I felt taken aback.

"So," she said, "I heard that your appeal didn't get off the ground—did you only just get out?"

Still feeling a touch shocked at the shift in tone, I replied, "That's right."

"They thought you were safe? No longer a danger to the general public?"

"I guess so."

Mercy made her lips pert. She nodded to the street behind me. "I need to get some lunch," she said. "I've only got another forty minutes or so." She cocked her head to one side. "Come with?"

I held myself still.

Unable to quite believe what was going on.

But I went along with it.

———

True to her word, Mercy led the two of us to a place called Starshine Café. They did takeaway sandwiches and other snacks. Mercy ordered a tuna-and-mayonaise baguette while I went with a BLT . . . unsure that my queasy stomach could handle anything more complex.

We shifted out of the café, and to a courtyard alongside.

The courtyard featured a fountain and was already well frequented by other office employees. Mercy waved to a group of them, but stopped short of going over to say hi.

As the two of us sat up on the edge of the fountain, I took in what Mercy was wearing: a simple, sleek black skirt which ended just above the knee. On top she wore a woolly jacket with the neck zipped right up to her throat.

For the first few minutes, the two of us just munched on our sandwiches in silence.

I guess we'd both worked up some hunger following the impromptu chase.

At first, Mercy attempted to hijack the conversation. She told me about where she lived, about the house she shared with her husband and her two daughters. She must've been paying close attention to me because she seemed to catch onto the fact that I didn't want to know.

When a silence opened up between us, I took my chance.

"What happened?" I said. "That day . . . with Petra? Why

did you all turn on me—why did you all *use* me?" I paused for a moment, trying to figure out if I should add anything, and I could only think of one thing. "It's been ten *years* . . . just how long can you hold onto a secret?"

Mercy popped the last morsel of her sandwich in between her lips, screwed up the paper sachet which the baguette had been delivered in. Then she tossed it into a bin across from us. Despite looking as if it might arc away and land on the ground, it slipped in right at the last moment.

What could explain that?

Luck?

Skill?

Practice?

Mercy munched her mouthful and then swallowed it down. She eyed me.

"It wasn't anything personal, Charlie," she said, for the first time actually saying my name. "You just happened to be there, a ready-made excuse . . . a ready-made *alibi*."

I focussed onto what she said. Made sure I understood it. *Really* understood it.

"You're," I started, still unsure, "You're admitting it?"

Mercy met my eye. Her smile was gone now. She held my gaze for several seconds and then a faint smile twisted the corners of her lips. "Come on, Charlie, like you said—it's been ten *years*, I think it's time to draw a line under the whole episode, don't you think?"

I wondered just what she meant by 'draw a line'.

Did she mean that I was supposed to write off the decade I'd spent in prison?

. . . *Right.*

Still, I could see my opening.

So I took it.

"Then what happened, what did you plan? *Why* was Petra killed?"

Mercy breathed in deeply. She brought her wrist up, glanced at her watch. "Listen," she said, turning back to me. "This is going to take some time, all right? How're you fixed after five o'clock, can you meet me after work?"

More than anything, I wanted to tell her, *No, I won't wait any longer*.

And yet, maybe it was her tone of voice, but she was being so reasonable.

There was no reason for me *not* to trust that she would tell me later.

Twists And Turns; A Blind Alley Or Two

I *finished one of the books* and started into the second while I waited for Mercy in the same park as that morning. My bench turned up free again and I scooted myself onto it.

The afternoon seemed to trickle by, and I couldn't help but feel that, with each moment, Mercy might be taking the opportunity to get further and further away from me.

She *would* fool me, wouldn't she?

She *would* take some back door . . . escape?

However, to my surprise, Mercy appeared in the doorway of the office building, clearly glancing around, searching for me. I folded the page and snapped my book shut, then crossed the street to meet with her.

As Mercy led me along the street, I was a little surprised when she looped her arm through mine, so the two of us walked as if we were schoolgirls. She brought us to a pub called *The Milk Churn*.

At the bar, she made a point of paying for the drinks,

muttering something along the lines of me having 'deserved' it . . . I said nothing in response.

I was beginning to believe that Mercy wasn't quite in control of her mental facilities.

I wondered if—*perhaps*—she had mixed up what 'prison' truly meant.

Getting through *prison* wasn't something you treated as a 'good job, well done'.

But Mercy seemed to treat it that way.

Despite my protests that I just wanted a fizzy drink of some description—nothing alcoholic—Mercy ordered us a pair of blue-coloured drinks in tall glasses. Both had bendy straws jutting out from within.

We took up a place in the corner of the bar.

Mercy withdrew a phone from her pocket and laid it flat on the table.

I still hadn't quite got used to that custom; the way that it'd become somewhat socially acceptable to skim through your phone while in company, but I'd observed the behaviour all the way on the train, and in all the restaurants, pubs, that we'd passed by.

Did people even *speak* to one another anymore?

Mercy sipped her drink down to about half-full almost immediately.

I took a tentative slurp at my own before taking a break.

It tasted vaguely of blueberries, but more of vodka and lime.

I couldn't honestly say I was a fan.

"So," I said, intent on not allowing Mercy to escape the theme. "What happened?"

Mercy eyed her mobile phone screen another second, then glanced up at me. "With Petra?" she said, smiling as if we were speaking about her latest crush, before adding—*just as nonchalantly*—"I killed her."

I was glad I hadn't taken a sip of the revolting drink because I'm sure I would've spat it right out. Still, I did feel my stomach sink. And my pulse rattled at my temples.

The only words I could get out were, "How? . . . *Why?*"

Mercy sipped at her drink casually. "Because we thought it'd work out best that way."

I felt the wrinkles form in my brow. "I . . . but . . . '*we*' ?"

Mercy waggled a finger at me. "You don't understand the dirt she had on us—on *all* of us."

"What 'dirt' ?" I said, unsure whether to be angry, outraged.

In the end, I was just plain *shocked*.

"You don't remember, do you?"

"Isn't that obvious?"

"A party . . . it was about a week before we set off on the trip." She paused, eyed me closely. "Do you remember?"

I shook my head. "No."

Mercy rolled her eyes. "We all turned up at a party, in *C* block, remember?"

I forced my mind back.

Thought about the week before the fieldtrip.

And then, with a lurch of my gut, I realised she was right.

"Remember?" Mercy said, again, slurping up the last of her drink. "Another?" she said, getting up from her seat and making for the bar.

She didn't give me a chance to say no.

————

Mercy returned from the bar, two fresh servings of the revolting blue drink in her hands. She set one of them down before me. I stared at its blue colour.

"Come on," Mercy said, flashing her eyebrows. "Drink up!"

She was referring to my first blue drink which I hadn't even got through a third of.

In truth, my head was swelling with an almighty pain. I didn't want anymore.

But needs must . . .

"Thought any more about that party?" Mercy said.

I had thought about the party.

I remembered how—when we'd walked in through the hallway of the building—I'd heard the rhythmic throbbing of bass. How I'd smelled the cigarette smoke on the air; mingled with marijuana. Something else there, too . . . though I couldn't be totally sure just *what*.

Some exotic substance I never got around to sampling.

The sheer quantity of people had been overwhelming. It'd been like setting foot in a basement club; it was the feeling that there was hardly a whiff of fresh air to be had in the entire place. I'd kept my eyes locked on Eric, who was in front of me . . . he had been following Alex and Petra.

Mercy and Graeme—I suppose—were behind me.

I wondered if even then they'd been making goo-goo eyes at each other.

Probably, knowing my lack of perception . . .

We'd gone up some floors, through the party—the people packed together. We'd travelled along a hallway; come to some-body's room . . . that was where the air was thickest with smoke.

I could remember that clearly.

But, anything else . . . any other *details* . . . they all seemed to fade into the fog of memory.

Lost.

I turned to Mercy, out of ideas.

"No?" Mercy said. "Not cottoned onto it?"

I shook my head. Because I felt compelled to, I reached for the blue drink, grasped it firmly, and then sucked on the straw. I grimaced without thinking. Thankfully, Mercy didn't seem to notice.

"At the party," Mercy said, "in one of those *rooms*; was the biggest drug dealer on campus.

A guy called Stan."

" 'Stan' ?"

She nodded. "Yeah, Stanislav—Polish."

"Like Petra?"

"Uh-huh."

Mercy slurped again on the straw . . . I noticed that the contents of the second blue drink were disappearing just as quickly as the first. She set the drink down and continued, "The day after that party, Stanislav got busted."

"Huh?" I said, still wrapping my head around my memory.

Still trying to recall these things for myself.

"Yeah," Mercy said, flashing her eyebrows.

Taking another slurp of her drink.

She set the glass back down, glanced at the screen of her mobile.

"Whole squad showed up . . . vans. *Armed* guys. You know, that sort. They estimated that he had close to half a million pounds' worth stashed there—in that room of his. Stan had been failing his university course for years, but he was doing terrific business out of it, apparently . . ."

"Wait," I said, involuntarily leaning across the table. "What's all this got to do with Petra? Where does she come into this?"

Again, Mercy held up a finger. As if I was supposed to be *silent*. "There'd been rumours," Mercy said. "Rumours floating about campus. About snitches. About these students the police had got hold of. Students that they *paid* to inform on others. Well," she added, taking another drink, "that's a fancy way of putting it. From what I heard, they were only encouraged to keep an eye out."

" 'An eye out' ?" I replied, feeling as if I was sinking now.

"Yeah," Mercy replied.

"And you think," I began, my throat suddenly feeling dry; a tremble starting to grip hold of my bones, "that Petra was one of those?"

Mercy nodded. "Yep. Without a doubt. Alex saw her bank statement once—guess she just left it out on her desk for anyone to see. There was a payment for a thousand pounds listed as something like 'Wilful Cooperation'." She waved her hand as if this detail wasn't important. "The truth was that she was a rat. She was the one who informed on Stan—the one who got him arrested."

"So," I said, "that was why—*why* you killed her?"

A smile twitched Mercy's lips. "That was one of the reasons . . . that was Eric's reason."

" 'Eric's reason' ?" I said, unable to grasp what was going on here.

Mercy nodded. "If you'll recall, Eric used to deal a little himself, you know, on the side. I guess that he was paranoid about having somebody hanging around—someone who was on police payroll, if you know what I mean?"

To be honest, I really wasn't sure what *any* of this meant.

But I was trying to put my mind to it . . .

———

Outside, I realised that night had fully set in.

From the state of the pub—from the amount of people clustered about the bar—I suddenly realised that it was a Friday. That it was the time for merriment; for celebration that the week was over and, for two days, it wouldn't be back again. I always found a certain sadness in Fridays . . .

I turned back to Mercy. "You said that Eric's reason for having Petra gone was because he was paranoid—worried that she might turn him in . . . what about the others?"

Mercy pouted, crossed one leg over the other. She eyed her second blue drink, only a trickle remaining in the bottom. Surely she wasn't considering ordering another one?

Perhaps working on a planning committee was more hectic than it sounded.

"What about *your* reason?" I said, pressing Mercy closer.

"I . . ."

But, apparently noticing somebody at the bar, she trailed off.

Waved to them.

For a sickening moment, I thought that Mercy might invite whoever she had spotted over to 'chat' with us . . . just what we would 'chat' about escaped me . . .

Thankfully, though, Mercy got over her waving and turned back to me.

She shrugged. "You saw the evidence—the interviews, didn't you?"

I noted a slightly sharp tone to her voice now.

She didn't seem as carefree—as *up*—as she had been just a few moments previously.

It all made me feel very unnerved indeed.

"The *transcripts*," Mercy added, hissing the 's'.

I thought back to all that time I'd spent with Daniella in the prison—all that *wasted* time. Yes, there had been the theory surrounding Mercy, and how she had, at first, denied that she'd had any sort of relationship with Petra before the fieldtrip; only to spill details during the interview process.

Details which weren't picked up, or which were chosen to be 'irrelevant' by whoever had carried out the investigation.

"Yes," I said, glancing down at my pair of blue drinks, one of them drunk down about a third of the way and the other entirely untouched.

Seeing the way Mercy was eyeing the full glass, I shifted it in her direction. She flashed a smile at me by way of thanks. Took it in her hand.

It was hard to believe I was in the presence of a killer; and, in fact, the more that I thought about it, the less I grew to believe that it was so. But Mercy had just *admitted* that she'd done it . . . what was I *supposed* to think?

"So," Mercy said, taking a sip from her third drink. "What did you find?"

I thought back to the research which Daniella had conducted, and which I had found some inconsistencies in . . . it had all been so long ago, and it all *did* seem irrelevant now.

I shook my head. "Just some parts . . . parts which didn't make any sense."

Mercy pouted. "Why not?"

"They didn't match up with your previous statements—your previous *versions* of events."

"Didn't they?" Mercy replied, not sounding half as surprised as she should have.

Already, she was halfway through with the drink.

A silence sunk in over us again, although the silence was all relative given the caterwauling going on over by the bar. "Mercy," I said, cutting through the silence, "why don't you just tell me the reason—the reason why you wanted Petra dead?"

She shrugged a shoulder. "She killed my cat."

Although I knew how melodramatic it might seem to the casual observer, I couldn't help but lean into her. ". . . *What?*"

For the first time, Mercy seemed as if she was showing off something approximating genuine emotion. Her eyes had gone watery. And her lower lip wobbled slightly.

It'd only taken two and three-quarters of those blue abominations to loosen her up . . .

This seemed the only part of the conversation where I could say, with any certainty, that she was telling the truth. But what did I know?

. . . I *had* spent the past decade with liars and thieves.

Mercy nodded to my question. "As I'm sure you saw in the transcripts, me and Petra were really quite close . . . for a while. We even used to do one another's hair, that sort of thing. Then, I don't know, there was this moment—this moment when she seemed to . . . *snap*."

" 'Snap' how?"

"Can't really explain it—it was like where we'd once been friends—where we'd once spent almost every spare moment in one another's company—we just began to drift apart. As if *she* wanted us to be strangers again. I think . . ." Mercy left this lingering for a few moments ". . . she was worried that I might be a threat to her—that I might be angling to take Alex away."

I shook my head at this, unbelieving. Then again, I hadn't known anything of Mercy and Petra's former friendship so who was I to judge?

Mercy swallowed back the last of the blue drink and then tilted it all the way down her throat until there was nothing left. I became aware that she was steadily eyeing what remained of my *first* drink . . . but this time I didn't see fit to offer her it. Somehow it seemed wrong.

"One day, when my family came up to visit, they brought my cat, Mr Tim."

" 'Mr Tim' ?" I said, somewhat beleaguered by this detail, though I couldn't say quite why.

She nodded dolefully. "They brought him up with them . . . and they found him . . . found him . . ."

I leaned in closer, as Mercy's voice got quieter and quieter. "Where? Where'd they find him?"

She shook her head.

A single tear rolled down her cheek.

She glanced up at me.

If she was trying to manipulate me then she was doing an awfully convincing job of it.

"In the microwave."

"What?" I said, unable to sit still now, perching on the edge of my seat. "How? Why wasn't that reported to anyone . . . why was . . ."

But I trailed away because Mercy was now sobbing into her palms.

I noticed somebody approaching us. I heard a husky, male voice over my shoulder.

"She okay?" he said.

I whipped around, shot off a fierce glare. "She's fine, *thanks*."

I continued to stare at the man, dressed in a black shirt unbuttoned to his chest hair, until he returned to the bar, to be among his friends, where he was loudly admonished for his pitiful attempt at 'picking up the pieces' . . . I had learned *that* tactic well at university.

I turned my attention back to Mercy.

She was still sobbing away into her hands.

Girls like Mercy always seemed to attract men like flies to sugar.

It took Mercy a few moments to get herself back together. She glanced up at me, her eyes meeting mine. "Ridiculous, don't you think?"

"I . . . I can't see how you can tell for sure . . . if . . ."

There was a flash of anger in Mercy's eyes—that, surely, would've been impossible to feign. She pounded the heel of her hand against the table. It sent the empty glasses clinking into one another.

"You don't *know!*" she said, almost shouting it.

I noticed a few heads turn in our direction.

Surely it was obvious to them that Mercy was drunk . . . and angry.

"You didn't *see* her," Mercy replied, quieter this time.

At least she wasn't quite at the level of drunk which completely stole away her sense of situation.

Mercy met my eye. "I saw her," she said, "I *know* that she did it."

"You didn't go to the police, you didn't . . ."

Mercy shook her head, with a wry smile. "No," she said, "because I knew that I could make it up in other ways—that there would be some way to get her back."

"Like throttling her to death with a hatchet?"

Mercy glanced to my drink again. "Are you going to finish that?"

———

Against my better judgement, Mercy cajoled me into buying another round of those blue drinks. I wondered if the barman was going to make some comment about Mercy—about chucking her out if she was going to make any more of a fuss—but all he gave me was a knowing flash of his eyebrows in the direction of where we were sitting. I don't quite know what else I expected to get out of Mercy—if I expected her to spill some more details . . . to tell me about Graeme and Alex, and why they'd entered a pact to kill Petra out in the wilderness.

And then frame *me* for it.

If I did expect that then I was soon to be disappointed.

Mercy fell deeper and deeper beneath the shadow of the alcohol. Her eyelids began to droop. Many more of the men at the bar looked over at us. I knew that the focus of our meeting had shifted. It had turned into victim and rescuer. It was my task, now, to get Mercy back home safely.

That was easier said than done, since, when I raised the prospect of going home Mercy rapidly downed her drink before signalling to the barman for another.

The barman, with a nonchalant shrug, did as she requested.

I watched on as she sank it without any visible fuss . . .

Finally, when Mercy agreed that it *was* time for us to leave, I helped her up from her seat. She staggered about all over. In my head, I tried to calculate how many drinks she'd had during our time at the bar, and I soon got myself lost. So I just gave up counting.

I did my best to keep Mercy upright as she leaned all her weight up against me.

Several times, I thought that she was going to wheel away from me; fall to the ground.

Land with a *thump*.

And that the two of us would have to spend a surreal period in Accident and Emergency.

Thankfully that fate was spared me.

We reached the taxi rank without any further drama.

Through narrowed eyes, Mercy scrutinised the cab drivers, deciding that she wouldn't go with any of the first ones . . . that she would only settle with the one fourth back on the rank. It took quite a good deal of convincing to get her to see that, really, it would be somewhat inconsequential *who* drove her home, just as long as *someone* did it.

With the taxi driver holding open the back door to the cab, and casting a somewhat dubious glance over us—no doubt worried about the state of the back seat following the trip— Mercy turned into me, pushed her face up too close, and said, "You know, Charlie, you're the closest thing I have to a friend now."

Mercy staggered a couple of steps away from me.

Vaguely in the direction of the opened door of the taxi.

As I watched her into the cab, giving me a frivolous, little-girl wave, I couldn't help but mutter under my breath, "You've got a funny way of treating your friends."

Another Blind Alley

A s I made my way back to the hostel I'd stayed at the night before, I turned my mind to Graeme, and how I was going to approach him. I wondered how much of what Mercy had said I could believe. If the veneer of what she'd said had been true—that there had been a pact between the others to kill Petra; and that, frankly, seemed the only thing which would've made any sense—then I surely had enough information to frighten Graeme with.

It was up to me how I would approach it.

How I would go after him.

Just as they had all gone after me . . .

On the computer in the hostel, I spent a good deal of time planning a route to Graeme's home. He lived to the south of London, in a small village. When I glanced over his internet presence, I immediately saw he wasn't as helpful in sharing his address. But there was enough to go on.

Enough for me to *find* him.

I turned in for an early night, and got up with the first light, as I had done the day before when I'd gone stalking Mercy. As I shoved on out of the hostel, a steady drizzle was trickling down so I was glad for the waterproof jacket I'd shoved in the bottom of my bag on a whim.

I tugged the hood up and plodded along the pavement.

It took a succession of Tube journeys before I arrived at a train station which would take me south. As I sat on the train, my forehead pressed up against the cool glass, watching as the grey skies pressed down upon the grim, grey cityscape, I wondered what I should expect from Graeme.

When I'd gone to see Alex he had been standoffish, but he had at least allowed me in.

Mercy, on the other hand, had run off the second our eyes had met.

What might Graeme do?

I supposed I was going to find out soon . . .

The village had one of those quaint, English-countryside names which I forgot immediately after seeing. I trudged along the winding road and past the semi-detached houses. The street was fancier than Eric's, but less extravagant than Alex's.

Graeme's house didn't have a number, only a name:

Bluebells

There was a single, porcelain plaque nailed to the brickwork beside the front door with the name and a bunch of bluebells painted on there. Since there was no doorbell, I used the brass knocker.

Listened to the percussive thud echo through the house within.

And then I waited.

Restraining the urge to tap my foot impatiently.

There was the *scrub* of footsteps from within, the sound of shoes over carpet, and I soon found myself staring back at a middle-aged lady wearing a turquoise tracksuit and brandishing a feather duster. I explained my predicament. And was told that the master of the house would not be home until that evening. That I was to return then.

There was no chance to skulk my way into the house, to have a nice little poke about the place, because the woman—the cleaner, apparently—promptly slammed the door shut in my face.

I turned, made my way back through the village and wondered what I was going to do next.

I'd brought along the two books which I'd purchased the day before. The tea room I'd spotted on the way to Graeme's house seemed a little *too* quaint for my tastes, so I gave it a wide berth.

Thankfully, there was a wooden bench set beneath a decent covering—a bus stop?—and I took refuge there, forking through my bag for the provisions I'd bought back at the train station.

I'd only been sitting on the bench for around twenty minutes when I heard a familiar voice.

Graeme's voice.

"Charlotte?" he said.

I turned to him.

Looked him over.

He wore a powder-blue shirt tucked into a pair of black jeans. His hair had grown out from the time when he'd been at university. There were a few daubings of grey. Everything about him seemed to have *shrunk*—no longer did he have the bulging muscles, and neither was there the sharp look in his eye.

Despite the drizzle, he wasn't wearing a waterproof coat. Rain speckled the shoulders of his shirt, and I was certain that he must've been nearly freezing to death.

When my eyes dived further south, I noted the wedding ring on his finger.

Apparently noticing my gaze, Graeme's eyes, too, shifted downwards.

So that both of us were staring at his wedding ring.

A short silence, then Graeme glanced back up.

He managed a sad, frail sort of smile. "I was, uh . . . just about to go and play some snooker."

"Snooker?" I replied, with disbelief.

He nodded in reply. "Would you like to come?"

Still somewhat blind-sided by the situation, I blinked back at him, managed to find a smile of my own and said, "All right."

———

'Snooker' turned out to be a small, dilapidated shed just off the main road.

From one of his jeans pockets, Graeme produced a key at the end of a large, splintered wooden fob. With a wry grin, he slipped the key into the hole, turned. As he pushed the door open, and stepped inside, bringing the musty air wafting out, he muttered, "Could do with a bit of a spring-clean, this place."

I held back, glancing around me, back to the village.

Nobody else around.

Everybody else *at work* . . . or so I imagined.

I stepped into the shed, a light blinking on as I did so.

Sure enough, I eyed the long table occupying the centre of the room.

A cloth was draped over the table, and beneath I could make out the forms of balls, scattered all across the surface.

"Do you play?" Graeme said.

Surprised at the question—surprised at the *situation*—I turned my head in his direction. He was already busying himself with chalking one of the cues he'd pulled from the wall rack.

"I'll just watch," I replied.

Graeme shrugged. "Suit yourself."

True to my word, I stood back and observed as Graeme went about the routine of peeling off the snooker table covering, folding it into a neat little bundle which he tossed down into the corner of the shed. He set up all the balls: the reds in the neat triangle; the yellow, brown and green all in a neat row; the blue, pink and black all at—apparently—well-calculated spots on the cloth. Finally, Graeme settled down, bringing himself flat with the snooker cue. He slid the cue back several times, judging with a single opened eye over the top of the smooth wood before— with a sudden, violent *jab*—sending the reds scattering with the white ball.

Apparently pleased with his work, he straightened up.

Stood back.

Glanced over at me.

He gave a slight smirk. "Easier with one person," he said. "Can just put my mind to potting all the balls I need to pot."

"Right," I replied, as Graeme prowled about the periphery of the table, sizing up his next move in this solitary game.

As he eyed up his next shot, he said, "I like coming here. Anybody in the village is welcome to use the table; we've all got a key." He paused, lined up a red for one of the middle pockets, and then, with that same, sudden *stab*, he fired the white ball after it.

The red bounced off the corner of the pocket.

He winced. "Bugger." And then, seemingly still affected by this failure, shaking his head as he straightened up, he repeated, "*Bugger.*"

As he went about chalking his cue again, he continued to address me. "There's something about the simplicity of snooker

—of see-ball, *hit-ball*—that just gets my mind off everything else. Something which gets my mind off the *world* . . ."

I watched on as Graeme trailed off, stalking his next move on the table.

He crouched down, breathed in deeply.

Although he was concentrating hard, I couldn't see any of that ruthless—*sharp*—competitive edge which'd been so alluring back at university. It seemed as if that 'sharpness' had truly been blunted for good. As he slid the cue back another time, bringing it sliding forwards with a deft flick of his wrist, he said, "Nothing like snooker to take your mind off worries."

"What sorts of 'worries' ?" I said, folding my arms across my chest, wondering whether I might've already crossed a line with this man . . . nothing more than an acquaintance, really.

Then again, I did suppose that he, along with three others, had been responsible for robbing me of over a decade. If anybody had licence to be *imprudent*, then surely that would be me . . .

However, judging by the direct manner in which Graeme answered the question, I really needn't have feared treading on any toes. "Losing the house," he said. "Wife's already gone . . . taken the kids." He snorted a laugh, his attention still directed down at the snooker table. "Cleaner came by today. When I heard her coming in, I hid. Forgot she was coming at all. Once she'd got in—got busy *cleaning*—I snuck out a back door. Came here." He shook his head, again with a sense of disbelief. "Don't have any cash to pay her with, that's the thing . . . I had hoped she might see there was no cash on the kitchen counter and head back out, but I suppose she thinks that I've just *forgotten* to leave it this week —that *next week* there'll be two weeks' worth of payment."

This time he chuckled.

But those dark circles beneath his eyes betrayed his weariness.

The look of a man who had, quite simply, *had enough* . . .

He looked back at me. "Guess she's in for a surprise, hmm?"

"Guess so."

"Yeah," he said, staring me back in the eye, and then looking down at the snooker table again, his mind no doubt alive with invisibly drawn geometry as he calculated his next shot. He bent down, slipped his cue back, and then prepared to fire the white ball again. Before he took a shot, he said, almost as an afterthought, "What're you here for, Charlie? What is it that I can help you with?"

I waited until the white ball *clacked* into a trio of reds, and then said, "I want to know about Petra—about what really went on . . . about who *murdered* her."

———

Graeme strolled about the table several times. He focussed down on the cloth, his eyes prying over each and every ball, apparently judging all of them on their merits. I began to wonder if he'd heard me at all, or if I was going to have to repeat myself. But he finally replied.

"Mercy," he said. "*Mercy* did it."

His tone was deadpan, emotionless.

And his expression hangdog.

I thought about what Mercy had said—how she had admitted to doing it herself.

. . . But I still didn't quite buy that.

It seemed too simplistic.

A *cat* for a *human being*?

But, then again, just how well did I think I knew Mercy?

As if we were speaking about anything at all—as if I hadn't

travelled down from Scotland to speak with him; and as if Graeme wasn't at some point of extreme crisis—he resumed his game, continuing to ping the balls about the table.

I wondered if he'd lost it somehow . . . if he'd lost his *mind*.

Although I was curious as to what Graeme did—what his *work* was—I didn't want to ask anything which might carry the risk of 'setting him off' in some way.

In making him turn violent.

But, then again, my central purpose for having come here—to visit—was hardly a light-hearted matter. Perhaps all the more reason to get it out of the way as soon as possible.

"Graeme?" I said.

"Mm?" he said, taking aim at the black ball now.

"I found those messages . . . the email on Eric's computer . . . the post on the message board; the one which was purporting to be from Eric *himself* . . . I know that you were up there, in Edinburgh, the day that Eric died."

Maybe I believed that Graeme would do something dramatic.

That he would slip taking his next shot, the cue tip tearing into the tablecloth.

That he would spin around.

Stare at me.

An expression of fury.

Snap his cue across his knee . . . advance on me with the broken pieces.

Ready to thrust them through my throat.

If he was planning on killing me—to wrap up all the loose ends—then I didn't believe he would find a better opportunity than this one, right now. But, instead, he just continued to play.

He took two shots—*three*—before he so much as deigned to look at me.

When he did, his expression was cool, calm, and I couldn't

help feeling that *I* was the one who was most at risk of losing control here. That *I* was the mental one.

"I had nothing to do with it," he replied.

I shook my head, feeling an itching sensation through my veins now.

A tightness forming across my chest.

"Graeme, the evidence is all *there* . . . you said that you'd be seeing him soon, that you were going to meet up *that day* . . ."

Graeme met me with a stone-cold glare.

I started to wonder if the bumbling, clumsy façade he'd greeted me with thus far had been just that. And he was only waiting to fathom my reason for coming—waiting to shock me with some sudden act of violence.

Unexpected.

Deadly?

"I hadn't anything to do with Eric," Graeme replied, decisively, crouching back down at the table. "I haven't set foot in Scotland since I graduated from uni."

Again, I knew this to be false.

But I waited until I could get all the facts.

If all else failed, then I knew I would go to the police, show them what I'd found. Although I really couldn't care less whether or not all three of them went to prison, what I *did* want was an admission of what they'd done. I wanted to be put in the loop.

Not cast aside, into the shadows.

"But the message . . ." I got out, my voice quivering slightly. "I *know* what I saw."

Graeme struck his hardest shot yet, sending the pink ball pinging to all corners of the table. When the ball whipped near to Graeme's hand, he reached out and stopped it dead with a single finger. He gripped hold of it. Held it in his fist. Stared at it.

For several seconds, he seemed to become lost in the apparent wonder of the ball.

I was on alert for him to toss it at me, at any second.

And readying to flee.

He turned his eyes onto mine, away from the ball. "What was it the message *exactly* said?"

For a long moment, I couldn't speak.

Something stuck in my throat.

I had read those messages over *so many* times that it was impossible for me *not* to speak the words. " 'I know we're meeting up today, in town.' "

I swallowed hard.

The only times that I'd ever learned stuff by memory, it was by repeating it over and over again to myself consciously . . . usually scribbling it out on a piece of paper.

But, in this case, that simply hadn't been necessary.

Just normal reading.

Just *normally* wanting to go over the information again and again—and *again*.

I went on. " 'I know you said that we weren't to speak about the plan like this. But I wanted to let you know about the decision I've taken, that I'm not going to stick to the arrangement any longer. Charlie doesn't deserve this. Nobody deserves this. I think it's time the truth came out. It's been long enough.' " I paused, thinking about adding the rest, and deciding that there was no reason *not* to. " 'Fair warning. Rick'," I finished.

Graeme stared deep into my eyes, that pink ball still clasped tightly in his fist. Outside the shed, I heard a car passing by. In the tranquillity of the village, it sounded almost like a cavalcade of tanks.

"And where," Graeme replied, "does it say that *I* was going to meet up with him?"

I shook my head. " '*We're* meeting up today . . .' "

Graeme continued to stare at me. A slight smile curled the corners of his lips. "I don't see where my name comes into it."

A chill entered my bloodstream.

My mind whirred.

I felt as if I was sinking.

Then I snapped back to the present moment.

"Who, then . . ." I got out. "Who was meeting up with Eric?"

"Who'd you think?" he said, turning his attention back downwards, onto the table once again.

I scoured my mind.

There was only one answer, of course.

"Alex?"

Graeme shrugged. "Guess that'd be it."

He took a shot, sending the final red ball into one of the pockets.

He chalked his cue.

Something seemed to have come over him now; a greater sense of gravity, as if he had returned to planet Earth once more. He glanced up at me. "Is there anything else?" he said. "Or have you come along here to *crow* it over me?"

I wanted badly to bite back against Graeme—to tell him that I had *every* right to 'crow it over him' if that was what I wished. After all, *I* was the one who'd gone to prison.

It wasn't my fault that he'd made a mess of his life while *I'd* been behind bars . . .

For several minutes, I just watched Graeme play.

Having potted the final red, he set about potting the other balls in sequence.

From the look of his posture, from his expert control of the white ball—the way he skidded it across the cloth, or else bounced it off the cushions at exact angles—made me think that he spent a great deal of time here; in this snooker shed.

Finally, I managed to get out my question. "Why did you want Petra dead? What *possible* reason could you have?"

Graeme paused, on the black now. He glanced up at me. Yanked his cue back. Then thrust it forwards. The black ball fizzed across the cloth.

Dropped, neatly, into the pocket.

———

"Hmm, let's see," Graeme said. "*What* possible reason could I have for wanting Petra dead?"

It took me aback that he was speaking so frankly; that he had no apparent fear that I might be wearing a wire. Or that there might be an unmarked police car parked down a nearby road, listening into every word of the conversation; just *waiting* for the incriminating detail before rushing into action.

"I don't know, Graeme," I said, folding my arms. "That's what I'm here for. To find out."

Graeme breathed in then exhaled harshly. "Who else have you been to see?"

Seeing no reason to hide the information, I told him.

Graeme stuck out his lower lip and tilted his head to one side.

Although the table was now clear of balls, he continued to stare down on the lush, green cloth; clearly lovingly preserved, despite its humble surroundings.

"Why'd you leave me till last?" he said, finally looking up.

I might've had other thoughts on my mind, but I didn't allow them to show.

"Just a practicality," I lied. "North to south."

If Graeme didn't buy this explanation, he made no reaction.

Perhaps he was stowing it all away for later, so that—at a moment's notice—he could hurl it back out at me . . . *expose* me in some way.

" 'North to south'," he repeated back, still staring at the green cloth.

"That's right."

He rested the rubber end of his snooker cue on the floor. He leaned the cue itself up against his thigh, and thumbed the sleekly varnished wood. "Petra," he said.

I added nothing to this, not wanting to break his flow.

"Mercy told you, didn't she?"

"About what?" I said.

"About Petra . . . and the *drugs*?"

I nodded at this. "She said that Petra was some sort of an undercover liaison for the police—that she thought *Petra* was the one who turned in that dealer . . . who was going to turn in Eric."

"Mm," Graeme replied.

I waited out the beats of my heart, wondering if Graeme was going to add anything else on his own. But I decided that I'd need to step in. "Was that it?" I said. "Were you involved in the drug-dealing too? Was that why you had to 'dispose' of Petra?"

Graeme remained very still. He was almost like an oil painting, standing there, beside the snooker table, looking pensive, the cue down at his side.

"Drugs?" he said, with a slight smirk. "Never did touch that stuff . . . not me."

"Okay, but then *what* was it?"

Graeme shifted to look me in the eye. "You remember coming into my room that time."

I stretched my mind back, trying to remember.

In fact, for some strange reason, it *was* memorable.

It was probably the only time I had ever been in Graeme's bedroom

The first and *last* time.

It'd been after a lecture on coastal erosion. I'd been trying to get away from the crush of people leaving the hall, and hadn't been able to . . . stuck in the bottleneck headed out.

It'd taken me aback when Graeme had appeared—*smiling*—beside me.

Asked if I'd like to go back to his room.

I'd thought it'd been an indecent proposal . . . though not an undesired one.

Soon after, though, it'd become apparent that this wasn't to be some spontaneous outpouring of passion. No, *not exactly*. Outside, in the cold light of day, I found Alex, and Petra, Mercy, too, if I remember rightly, all standing and waiting for Graeme.

Together, with my heart dying just a touch, we'd all made our way to Graeme's bedroom.

And then we'd sat on the edge of his bed.

Each of us with a beer.

And it being barely three o'clock in the afternoon.

I shook my head.

Returned to the present.

Graeme met my eye, like Mercy before him, willing me to remember some particular detail; willing himself to simply make the memory *appear* within my own mind.

But there was nothing there . . . at least nothing that I found remarkable.

Graeme replaced the snooker cue in the rack. Then he slowly made his way around the table. He stopped when he was half a dozen paces away from me.

I snatched another glance at the door.

Thought about running.

"The beer," Graeme said, his eyes now one-hundred-per-cent focussed on mine. "Do you remember the *cold* beer?"

I nodded that I did.

"Where did the beer come from?"

I was about to shake my head—even ready to laugh out loud at this *odd* question—but then I snapped onto what Graeme wanted me to remember.

I looked back at him. "The mini-fridge."

Graeme held his hands up in surrender as if this explained *everything*.

"Sorry," I said, "I don't get it."

"Remember when Petra finished a beer? Remember when she laid it at her feet?"

"Yeah . . ." I replied.

"What did she do then?"

I shook my head. "Went over to the mini-fridge—got herself another one?"

Graeme smiled, thickly . . . again, as if this explained *everything*.

"And?" I said.

"You don't see it?" Graeme said, his expression transforming, becoming somehow *troubled* . . . "You don't see *why? How?*"

"No."

Graeme sighed.

Took a couple of steps closer to me.

"Listen," he said.

I could feel the warmth of his breath now.

"You know that I was a rower . . . you at least know *that* much?"

"Uh-huh."

"And you know that I was *serious* about it . . . that I'd gone

226

training nearby . . . that I'd often head back down south at weekends?"

I decided it was better not to tell him that this was all news to me.

"Right," I said.

"There wasn't just *beer* in that mini-fridge."

I took a few moments to absorb just what he was insinuating.

And then, all at once, it struck me.

When I turned to face Graeme, I was surprised at how close he was.

"You were . . . *using?*"

Graeme stared me back in the eyes.

Took another step closer still.

Then, solemnly, he nodded.

"*Somehow,*" he said, putting extreme stress on the word, "my coach got wind of it. Next time I went down south, I got *tested* . . ." He flurried his hands. "Out of *nowhere.* That was the end of it for me. Tossed off the team. Name tarnished." He held up his index finger to better demonstrate this point. "One time, that was all it took."

I stared back at him.

His eyes filling mine.

He took one more step forwards, then reached out, brushed my crossed forearms with his fingertips. "You know," he said, "I always found you kind of . . . *sexy*, back at university . . . I always thought . . . always *wondered* if you just might feel the same."

A quiver passed over the surface of my skin.

My gut clenched.

It was strange—standing there—ten years since I'd had any sort of male contact of this nature, to find myself rendered utterly *paralysed* by it.

The sensation only lasted a moment.

I took a step back.

Tried to wriggle my way away from him.

But he took another few steps forwards.

Grabbed hold of my wrist.

Twisted it. *Painfully*.

"Let go!" I got out, through gritted teeth.

He grabbed me harder still.

I waited . . . knowing I would only get one chance.

Graeme's new body—his apparently *weedy* frame—was deceptive. He could still easily overpower me. "Come on," he said, his voice a murmur now, almost like a young boy's cloying tone. "Come on, come on . . ."

I took my chance.

As he took another step into me, as he brought another hand around to seize hold of my arm, I intercepted him, thrust him back—and *away* . . .

I ducked quickly beneath his arm as he brought it down on me.

Attempting to *swipe* hold of me.

But he was too slow.

I guess all the snooker in the world wouldn't do much for his reflexes.

Before he could get close to me again, I was at the door.

Then out.

Into the drizzle, falling harder now.

I broke into a run. If Graeme did attempt to pursue me, then he soon gave up.

When I reached the train station—when I glanced back over my shoulder—he was nowhere to be seen. I sighed out the stress of the situation, turned my attention up to the departure times, and then got on the first train heading back to London.

Back North

There *didn't seem* to be much point in me returning to the hostel.

I thought that I had everything I needed.

So I caught the first train out of King's Cross, going back up to Edinburgh.

In retrospect, I had to admit that my trip had been mostly productive.

I had found out Petra's killer, after all.

And I'd learned of Mercy and Graeme's motive . . . of *why* they'd wanted to cover it up.

A dead cat.

And a ruined sports career . . . though, in truth, if Graeme had really believed he was ever going to make it as a professional rower then it seemed strange to me that he would've decided to attend the University of Inverness instead of Oxford or Cambridge . . .

I was beginning to see that there might've been a sense of delusion at Graeme's heart.

Something which would turn *nasty* if challenged.

I believed I'd caught a glimpse of that nastiness in the snooker shed.

What would he have done if I hadn't protested?

I tried not to think about it.

I tried not to think at all . . .

I used my bag as a pillow, wedging it into the gap between the seat and the wall of the train carriage. Although I dozed for a while, I couldn't quite find a deep, soothing sleep.

There was, quite simply, too much going on in my mind for that.

I was putting all the pieces of the puzzle together.

Trying to work out what they might mean.

I thought about what Graeme had said . . . about how that message I'd seen on Eric's computer hadn't insinuated the two of them would meet up in Edinburgh that day . . . that it had, in fact, meant that Eric and *Alex* would be meeting up.

I knew I wouldn't be able to pass through Edinburgh *without* paying Alex another visit.

It was impossible to stop myself yawning as I trod along the streets of Edinburgh, headed for Alex's house. It felt as if the world wasn't quite real any longer—as if it had become *dampened* by all that I had learned of my 'friends'.

Somehow, I suppose, I'd harboured the hope that there would be some sort of a logical explanation for what had gone on . . . some *logical* explanation for my friends' deeply illogical behaviour on Loch Monar. Was that too much to hope for?

The only piece which was missing was Alex. I had to know if he had killed Eric . . . if he had killed Eric so that he wouldn't give everything away.

This time, when I rang the doorbell to Alex's house, it was a woman who came to the door. Although she was surely around my age, she somehow seemed much older. Perhaps it was the smart blouse she wore; how she had pearls strung about her upturned collar; a fine woollen cardigan draped over her shoulders.

When I asked after Alex, she looked me up and down—as if it was an offence for me to even have asked the question. Then it became obvious what the issue was.

She even spelled it out for me. "Is it you?" she said. "The one who's been keeping him from his family? Have you come here to apologise?"

I shook my head. "Sorry," I replied. "I really have no idea what you're talking about."

With an anguished sigh, she rolled her eyes, tilted her head back. When her eyes returned to mine, I noted the anger. "You have no idea what you've *done* to us . . . *all* of us . . ."

"Look," I said, attempting to cut through her, "I'm not who you think I am—I'm an old university friend of Alex's, and I . . ."

Before I could say anything more, the woman lurched forwards, off the doorstep, and struck me with a slap across the cheek.

It stung like nothing else.

Apparently just as shocked by this show of violence as me, she backed up onto the step, her eyes wide, and her lips slightly parted. "He's staying at a hotel. I'm sure you can find out *from him* which one."

The woman—apparently Alex's wife—made to shut the door.

But—pain seemingly no longer an object—I jammed my foot in the gap to keep her from closing me out. Alex's wife didn't try *too hard* to squash my foot.

And for that I was thankful.

"Please," I said, still reeling from the slap across my cheek. "Will you just tell me where Alex is—where he's *gone* to?"

Alex's wife eyed me through the gap. And then said, "*The Poulton Arms*—now take your foot out of my doorway or I shall be forced to call the police."

I did as she requested and the door slammed promptly shut in my face.

As I walked away from Alex's house, I speculated about how —following my first visit to him—I couldn't possibly have envisioned a more frosty reception. Well, that had just been it.

———

Since I hadn't a smartphone, and thus no handy internet access, I had to resort to asking people on the street for directions to *The Poulton Arms*.

Thankfully the kind people of Edinburgh soon had me steered in the right direction.

I think the best word to describe the place was 'posh'.

One of those hotels which seemed to have glittering brass furnishings, marble floors, and lobby boys all over. I felt extremely out of place walking to the reception desk to ask after Alex.

The receptionist—a blond girl in her early twenties—rang up to his room, told him who I was . . . I wasn't going to lie to him about who I was . . . that I was Alex's *theoretical* mistress.

If he didn't want to see me, if he truly wished to turn his back on the past, then that was his agenda. Thankfully, though, the receptionist told me he would be right down, and that I could wait in the lobby; the latter she kindly indicated with a gesture.

I took up my place in one of the bulky, squashy armchairs. It was one of those armchairs with arms large enough to seat an entire family on. The window looked out onto the street, and I could tell, from the slightly tinted hue, that it was one-way glass . . . so that those staying at the hotel could observe those passing by in the street without fear of discovery. I don't quite know why I was thinking of them in disparaging terms seeing as I was doing exactly the same.

When Alex arrived in the lounge, he looked just as bad as I might've imagined someone recently chucked out on their ear to look. He had a dejected expression. A whole week of stubble . . . the kind that'll take another week to turn into any sort of a beard not worn by students or the homeless.

He said nothing as he trudged past me, dumping himself into the armchair opposite.

For several moments, he slouched there, staring at me from out of the bottoms of his eyes, as if he might be able to magic me gone. Seeing as Alex wasn't going to do any talking, I decided to step in. "I went to see Mercy and Graeme."

"Mm," Alex replied, barely acknowledging that he'd heard me.

"I found out why . . . why they did it."

This time Alex said nothing, not even another one of those grumbles.

I decided this was permission, of a kind, to continue.

"I just came here wanting to know why you did it." I paused, for an awfully long time, then glanced around me. Even though I saw no one, I dropped my voice to almost a whisper. "And I wanted to know if you killed Eric."

Perhaps I expected some sort of a boggle-eyed reaction from Alex—for him to leap up out of his seat and to rush for me . . . for my *throat* . . . intent on doing me away.

But, instead, he just remained where he was.

Seemingly unmoved by my interrogation.

Finally, with a slight yawn, and a glance in the direction of the lounge bar—it was shut—he propped himself up in the armchair. He continued to stare at me, then said, "I didn't kill *anyone*."

"Then tell me," I said, "about those messages, on Eric's computer."

Alex held himself still.

He stared back into my eyes.

In that same detached manner which Graeme had managed.

I just hoped that—like Graeme—he wasn't about to make an advance on me . . . at least this time I had lots of people around.

"Listen," Alex said, perching on the armchair now, his fingers interlocked, "Eric was an enigma." He lifted a hand upwards, over his head. "Some days he was *up*"—he brought his hand downwards, to below his stomach—"and others, well, he was *down*."

"That doesn't explain the evidence," I said.

Alex shook his head. "It's all circumstantial, can't you see that? You know, he'd come to me, wanting to turn us—*all of us*—in." He sighed out hard. "I'd explained to him that it was too late —that too much had gone on for us to simply *change* our story, to scratch everything we told the police and make up something fresh."

"To tell the *truth*," I put in, feeling not a little pleased with myself.

Alex held up his hands in surrender.

At least it was an admission, of a kind.

"Look," he said, focussing back on me, "that day, it's true, what you read into the email, that I was meeting with Eric . . . that was probably why I was the first to find him."

"How?"

Alex shook his head. "We were going to meet at a café, just

around the corner from where Eric lived. And so I went there
—*waited*—but he didn't show up. So I got up, walked around the
corner, thinking that Eric had forgotten . . . or"—again, Alex
threw his shoulders wide in a shrug—"that he'd gone and slipped
off into one of his moods."

These moods—*Eric's moods*—had never been quite apparent
to me.

But, then again, he had smoked an awfully large quantity
of weed.

Surely that might've been a red flag?

"The front door was unlocked," Alex went on, "and there
was only some mongrel for security. If I remember rightly, it
licked my hand all the way up the stairs."

I thought about Sammy.

Felt—strangely, *out of place*—like I wanted to smile.

But now wasn't the time for smiling.

"When I got to the top of the staircase I knew something was
wrong. Everything was just so . . . *quiet*." He shook his head. "It's
hard to explain, but I peeped in on Eric's bedroom, saw him
there, with the . . ."

Here Alex began to choke himself up.

The words simply couldn't make it past his throat.

It took a few minutes before he was able to continue.

"Anyway," he went on, "I left the house behind, got out
of there."

"Why didn't you go to the police?"

"Please," Alex said, with a wry smile, "don't you think that
they'd be just a *little* suspicious to find someone with *my* history
showing up like that?"

"I don't know," I replied. "You guys all seem to be the
experts."

Alex glanced out the window, to the pedestrians passing by. "I had nothing to do with it, you know, Eric was just a ticking time bomb."

"Like Petra," I put in.

Alex continued to stare out of the window, to the people passing by.

And then he finally replied.

"Like Petra," he agreed.

———

When the lounge bar finally did open, I ordered an orange juice while Alex went for something which looked much darker—*much stronger.*

We talked about strangely *normal* stuff for about half an hour before I felt comfortable about bringing Petra up again. I judged it by the state of Alex's glass—by how much the liquid within had diminished. If he was anything like Mercy, I knew it would work less as a truth lubricant, and more as a truth *serum.*

"What was the reason?" I said. "Why did Petra have to die?"

There were more people in the lounge now; a couple chatting animatedly behind us.

A family of five over in the corner.

But I was certain they were all far too wrapped up in their own conversations to pay us any sort of attention.

Alex laid his glass down on the table, breathed in deep, looked out the window again. "She was everything to me," he said. "*Really*"—he smiled—"you have no idea *how much* she meant to me."

"So," I said, "*why* did you do it?"

Alex screwed up his forehead as if this was something which required deep thought, as if this was something that he *hadn't* thought about over and over again throughout the years.

236

How *could* he forget something so vital.

Something which'd—*surely*—touched his life so totally, and in every way.

Something which, I imagined, had been responsible, in part, to the dissolution of his marriage.

When Alex met my eye again, he spoke clearly—*plainly*—but not on the topic which I had asked after. "You went to my house, didn't you?"

"Yes."

"My wife, was she there?"

I flashed my eyebrows. "Oh yeah."

Alex went quiet for a long while.

Looked out the window again.

"She has some funny ideas," he said. "Funny ideas about our marriage—funny ideas about what I've been doing."

I stayed silent, not feeling as if Alex's Marriage was a subject on which I was qualified to comment. It didn't feel as if Alex was searching for comments in any case. More like he was looking for someone to 'unload' on.

I wondered if Alex had many friends.

If he had anybody at all to confide in.

. . . If he was having to unload on me, then I supposed he didn't . . .

Alex took another sip from his drink, looked back to the bar, and I wondered if he was going to get another one for himself—and for me . . . à la Mercy.

But he held still.

Stayed rooted in his seat.

Alex grimaced slightly, staring into the dregs of his drink. "I remember one day, in the library, I was going through—looking for a book." He glanced up at me, met my eye briefly. "I saw you sitting there, poring over something or other, taking notes."

I tried to recall the memory, like Graeme and Mercy had prompted me to do before, but—*like before*—I couldn't summon the recollection.

And there was a reason why.

These were all simple, generic moments.

Hundreds of them every day.

How was *I* ever meant to know how much they'd touch the lives of others?

That, in the day, there would be an unexpected darkness?

Lurking.

One which I could never see.

Never understand.

"I asked you," Alex continued, mercifully not requesting that I fill in his memory of the day, "I asked if you'd seen Petra about anywhere. I'd been calling her up, but getting nothing but voice mail. Nothing but a recorded message." He paused for a long moment, the words getting trapped in his throat. "Finally, you told me that you'd seen her, with another boy, some *boy* from her course."

I stretched my mind for that day.

But found nothing.

Again, only darkness.

Husks of memory.

Alex went on, "I . . . I . . . don't know . . . it was about two weeks, three, before the fieldtrip—before *our* fieldtrip . . . and, well, I was speaking with Graeme and Mercy one day, all of us planning. And I confided in them." He sniffed a laugh. "Don't know why—I guess I had nobody else to confide in. I told them that I *thought* Petra was seeing someone else." He shook his head. "That was when Mercy pitched in, told me that I was right to be suspicious, and that, what was more, she had proof." He breathed out a heady sigh, then added, "It must've been the worst thing I've ever done—in my *entire* life . . . but once they'd begun telling me about their plan; and that Eric, too, was involved, there didn't seem any other option." He pursed his lips. "No escape."

I waited out a few more moments, in the vain hope that he would add something else of interest, but, it seemed, he had nothing else to say. Then again, what else did I want to *know*? He'd told me, in plain terms, that he, Graeme, Mercy and Eric had planned Petra's murder, weeks before.

I finally did come up with something of my own to add.

"What about me?" I said. "What did you *hope* from me?"

Alex met my eye once again. He reached up, adjusting his glasses so that they were once more level across the bridge of his nose. "There was no other option, Charlie, it was the only obvious way out. For all of us."

"So," I went on, trying to keep my tone of voice level—*reasonable*, "all that flip-flopping, all that time when you were putting *off* reporting Petra's murder, that was so you could tie up the loose ends concerning me . . . so that you could make *me* out to be the murderer?"

Alex nodded solemnly, then looked away. "The day when the drifter approached you, with the hatchet, handed it to you, it was Eric who handed over those items for the drifter to give to you. We agreed that all of us would be equally culpable; that we would *all* take responsibility." He gave a shrug, the hint of a smile. "In some way—*somehow*—it seemed the right thing to do . . . as if we'd be saving the four of us for the cost of the two of you."

My vision blurred.

I blinked several times.

Tried to bring Alex straight.

But he'd gone all wonky about the edges.

In the end, I suppose I must've said goodbye to him somehow, though I couldn't recall having muttered so much as a word. When I got up, left the hotel, and Alex, behind, I felt almost as if I was floating . . . as if my bones—my *body*—had become weightless.

It was only outside, back being buffeted by the biting, icy wind, that I felt my mind being cast back to that day. To the *week* we'd spent on Loch Monar. And, still, I couldn't quite bring myself to admit it had all really played out as it had.

Everything *still* seemed so surreal.

And yet, it *had* happened.

What was more, *I* was the one who'd taken the fall.

In The Day, Darkness

Back home, back in Inverness, I expected to find myself
barraged with recollections of those odd hazy days. I
thought that I would find myself traumatised by the time I'd
spent in prison; the time when there had been hope, and then
there had been none at all.

But there was nothing there . . . nothing but *numbness*.

I told no one else about what had *really* happened on Loch
Monar; from the looks of things, the way that my 'friends' lives
had all panned out, I couldn't rightly say that they *deserved* to be
thrown into prison—as I had been . . . to have their lives made
that smidgen worse. To punish not just themselves but their families too.

No, I couldn't do that.

The revelation came to me after some bang average day.

I'd got a part-time job in a local library—just around the
corner from my mother's house. My only other work companion
was a widow, Mrs Yorath, who would often proudly proclaim that
she had been running the library for nigh-on fifty years.

Whether or not this was true, I didn't pry.

It being near the end of the evening—just gone seven thirty; the library's closing time—I cast a glance in Mrs Yorath's direction, saw that she was dozing away at the counter. The barcode scanner still clutched firmly in her fist as if a reader might burst on through the door at any moment and demand to check out an item.

I'd finished reshelving the books that'd been returned that afternoon, and I woke Mrs Yorath to ask her for the next day off. In a sleepy haze, she'd told me that it was 'Fine, just fine' and I'd taken this as my cue to skulk off out into the autumn skies.

As I did up the toggles on my coat, gazing out to the fading light at the rim of the horizon, I couldn't help but find myself back there; on Loch Monar.

I could breathe in the heather, the Scots pines.

Feel those pebbles beneath my toes.

. . . Taste the blood in my mouth.

Hear the retches as those who had killed Petra confronted what they'd done.

Perhaps it isn't true what they say, that 'time heals all wounds'.

At least not for me.

It was as I plodded along the cobblestones, with no distraction to keep my mind away from the past, that I found myself thinking about how the others had got it into their heads to murder Petra.

Eric . . . *paranoid* about having his small-time drug-dealing busted.

Mercy's cat . . .

Graeme's promising rowing career, or—at least—what he'd *believed* to be a promising rowing career.

Then Alex . . . the one who had claimed to have loved her,

and yet, like all the others, been happy to play an active role in her death. Whether or not he'd been the one to wield the hatchet, it made no difference.

And then there was me; the naïve innocent. The one who would take the fall.

In the long hours I'd had to think at the library, I'd studied all my memories of those occasions the others had described to me. Those 'flash-points' which'd apparently led to the inevitability of Mercy *having* to die. The first, the party, and the drug dealer, Stan.

It had returned to me.

I remembered returning from the party, leaving the others behind. I'd—*somehow, from somewhere*—got hold of a spliff. And, alone, as always seemed to be the case, I was trudging my way back to my university bedroom.

I can still recall the steady flash of blue lights.

Police.

Even though I hadn't put the pieces together totally in my addled brain, I could plainly recall the uniformed officers asking me what I had. And how they'd asked me where I'd got it.

I would've liked to say that I was paranoid, that the cannabis had addled my mind—stopped me from thinking clearly. But, in truth, I know that the same thing would've happened had I been stone-cold sober . . .

I'd told them.

The address.

Everything.

They'd nodded, then driven off in their car.

Caught Stan.

And fired up the others' suspicions.

Made them *believe* that Petra was to blame.

When, all along, it had been me.

Next, I'd turned my mind onto Mercy's cat, and her story of how it'd been *Petra* who'd killed him . . . put him in the microwave . . . Mr Tim . . .

It was strange to think that I hadn't heard the story before.

I suppose it'd been kept low-key. Mercy hadn't gone to the police.

Again, I could recall having wandered through Mercy's building that day, and I had noted a youth from the village. One of those many kids with a shaved skull and a constant, mean-looking expression. He'd been twelve, thirteen, and clearly out of place there . . . but *I'd* said nothing about him; just allowed him to wander on into the building.

Could he have been the true killer?

The more I thought about it, the more I began to believe that it made sense.

And, in a way, it made me responsible for the death of Mercy's cat.

Or—at the very least—*more* responsible than Petra.

Alex had already told me that it was my story of Petra being with another boy which'd first made him suspicious; which'd driven Graeme and Mercy to lie to him.

Graeme was the last one which left me in doubt.

I thought about those substances, in his mini-fridge.

I *had* seen them.

And, what was more, I could clearly recall, when I'd been leaving a lecture one day, that I'd turned to one of my course mates—the two of us eyeing up Graeme in an *especially* tight sleeveless top—and told her that nobody got a body like that *au natural.*

. . . That there had to be a *little something* extra.

When my course mate had pressed me for a further explana-

244

tion, of just what I was getting at, I'd stated, flat out, that I'd seen those vials in Graeme's mini-fridge.

Had my course mate then gone on to tell others?

To reveal the truth?

To *spoil* Graeme's rowing future?

I couldn't help but believe.

As I crossed the River Ness, and stared down into the grisly grey waters, I couldn't help but imagine seeing Petra just below the surface. Her staring up at me. Clawing at me with her hands. Silently—*silently*—screaming for me to help . . . to see this plot which threatened to ensnare the both of us . . . the plot which would see her pay with her life, and me with my time.

But I hadn't seen.

I'd had my eyes firmly squeezed shut.

And, as I plodded on further, thinking about what I might do with my day off—perhaps take a walk out in the wilderness, alone—I couldn't help but wonder what else I might've missed in the world. What else I might be missing *now*.

Had I really been all that naïve?

Hadn't the clues been there if I'd *truly* wanted to see them?

. . . Again, and again, I knew that the answer could only be one thing.

And that answer—as all the very darkest, and cruellest of answers often are—was yes.

An unequivocal, *emphatic* yes.

THE END

Author's Note

Thank you for taking the time to read one of my books. If you would like to hear about my latest releases you can sign up for my newsletter here: www.aviain.com

Thanks for reading!

AV Iain

In The Day, Darkness
A Novel

www.ingramcontent.com/pod-product-compliance
Lightning Source LLC
Chambersburg PA
CBHW031317280626
47169CB00019B/2082